Starting with non-fiction, **Dianne Drake** penned hundreds of articles and seven books under the name JJ Despain. In 2001 she began her romance-writing career with *The Doctor Dilemma*. In 2005 Dianne's first Medical Romance, *Nurse in Recovery*, was published, and with more than twenty novels to her credit she has enjoyed writing ever since.

Also by Dianne Drake

Tortured by Her Touch
Doctor, Mummy...Wife?
The Nurse and the Single Dad
Saved by Doctor Dreamy
Bachelor Doc, Unexpected Dad
Second Chance with Her Army Doc

Sinclair Hospital Surgeons miniseries

Reunited with Her Army Doc
Healing Her Boss's Heart

Discover more at millsandboon.co.uk.

HER SECRET MIRACLE

DIANNE DRAKE

MILLS & BOON

To all my open-heart patients.

You were my inspiration
to be the best nurse I could be.

PROLOGUE

AS NIGHTS WENT, this was a beautiful one: still warm enough to enjoy being outside, with only a faint wind and the nip of a chill settling in. In the distance, Sapporo's snowcapped mountains stood tall and inviting, giving Eric that feeling that he could stay here, someplace different, someplace else. Someplace where there was time for this…for daydreaming, thinking about a future, having fun in his life. But it was up to him to let it in. Unfortunately, he'd never quite discovered how. But someday…

"Are you enjoying the seminar, Dr. Hart?" asked Dr. Michiko Sato, stepping up to the balcony rail next to him. Her seductiveness nearly blended into the night. Dark skin, black dress. All woman. He'd spent two days listening to her lectures, the dulcet tones that made the field of physiatry sound almost as sexy as she was. There were other lecturers, of course. But he only had ears for Michi. And eyes. *Especially* eyes. And he, as well as other experts in attendance, couldn't get enough of her smile, the way she turned her gaze downward as if she was shy…and her body to die for. But, most of all, her dedication and intelligence.

Dear lord, perfection in his view for only a few short days. Michiko Sato was a woman who interested him in so many ways, and for a man who couldn't let himself be interested it was damned frustrating. Especially since he'd caught her staring at him a time or two, and it had not been a professional stare. Well, damn it. He'd done this to himself, hadn't he? Drawn his boundaries and stayed behind them. Lived a life without the interruption of real pleasure. And now here was real pleasure standing next to him and it was all he could do to keep his hands from shaking.

"It's a very good seminar. And call me Eric, please." He twisted to see the full length of her, and the sight of Dr. Sato in something more than her professional garb—white lab coat—caught him off guard, even though he'd been watching her for nearly an hour now. Tonight, she was stunning in her black sleeveless dress with its low-cut neckline and a side slit nearly up to her hip. The dress was not too tight to be indecent, but tight enough to show her curves. And what fine curves they were. Curves that would fit him so well if ever he got the chance.

"Eric. And I'm Michi." She moved closer to him, brushed against his arm, and stayed there rather than stepping away. "You've been sitting in the front row, I've noticed. Every lecture, every day. Should I be flattered?"

"I have." He chuckled. "All the better to see you." That was a bold statement, but a coziness was settling in around them, and it seemed to be calling for a bold move. Especially since after tomorrow he'd be gone, and she'd be on to her next lecture group or back to her medical practice.

"Did you like what you saw, Eric? And what

you see right now?" She stepped away ever so slightly, to give him a better look.

"If I didn't, I'd have been sitting in the back row. The front row was never my style." She stepped into him a little more, and seemed so innocent doing it. But this wasn't innocent. They both knew where it was heading. He'd known it the instant he'd walked into her lecture hall and made eye contact with the most beautiful woman he'd ever encountered. There was destiny here. Maybe not one that would go beyond tonight, but it was inevitable. She knew it as well as he did.

"I'm glad you weren't. I think I was enjoying my view as much as you were enjoying yours."

Sliding his arm around Michi's waist, he pulled her as tightly to him as she could possibly get. "You don't mind, do you?" he asked.

"Not at all." She nudged her foot against his. "Not at all."

Then he pointed to the evening shadows of the mountains. "There's a little cabin up there. A very isolated cabin. My father owns it, and when I was a kid, he'd have a personal ski instructor bring me here to teach me how to ski. It was the only time I ever got to do something fun, just for the sake of doing it."

"So, you're a good skier."

"Depends on your definition of good, I suppose. In my day I was."

Michi laughed. "In your day? From what I've been seeing, you're still in your day, and it's looking quite good." She sat her glass of champagne down on the wall surrounding the third-story veranda and turned to Eric. "So, tell me, Eric, what else were you good at, in your day?" She wrinkled her nose and her eyes sparkled with flirtation. *"Or night?"*

He was good at being a surgeon, day and night, but that wasn't the way he wanted this conversation to go. Not after listening to her and watching her so intently for what seemed like forever. Memorizing her movements, anticipating her words, trying not to be distracted by her beauty yet being distracted by every little thing about her—the raising of an eyebrow, the slightest hint of a smile meant only for him. "I'm good at picking up your signals."

"And what are these signals telling you?"

"That tonight's our last chance. Tomorrow we'll both be back in our normal lives." Why was his attraction to her so strong? There'd been other women in his life, other opportunities, but tonight, with Michi…

"And just what would that last chance include?" she asked him.

"We have options," he said. "Dancing, although I'm not very good at it. We could go for a walk. Or, stay here and talk."

"Talking's overrated," she said. "And these shoes are definitely not made for walking or dancing."

He glanced down, noticed that her shoes were strappy and spiky, and while he was no expert, he couldn't imagine that what she was wearing was going to make a walk much fun. Yet while he thought they were probably uncomfortable as hell, they also looked sexy as hell, making her incredibly long legs seem even longer. "Then maybe you'd like to go sit someplace where you can take off those shoes. They've got to be killing your feet."

Michi laughed. "So, you're a practical man."

"That's what my colleagues tell me."

"That's what my aunt told me when she recommended you to this seminar. That you're good at your job, not always as sociable as you could be, and that you're governed by practicality. But the best in your field."

"Your aunt?"

"Agnes Blaine."

He knew Agnes. She worked on the medical end of cardiology while he worked on the surgical end of it. Specifically, pediatric cardiac surgery. "Small world," he said.

"Not really. I'm trying to grow my practice in different ways, incorporate more physiatry into medical and surgical areas where it's not yet used. I asked her to send someone who might be able to make use of my specialty. And while I wasn't specific in terms of what kind of specialty I wanted to approach, she thought cardiac surgery and rehab would be good. Hence…you. So, let's get back to these shoes. Are you offering a foot massage?"

"For starters."

"Then what?"

He bent over and whispered something in Michi's ear that caused her to laugh. "That sounds very naughty," she said.

"Well, if you think that's naughty…" He whispered something else in her ear, but this time he grazed her earlobe with his tongue, causing Michi to gasp, then stand on tiptoe and whisper something back to him.

"Will that get me a passing mark in your class?" he asked.

"That, Doctor, will send you straight to the head of the class."

"My favorite place," he said, picking up her glass of champagne. "And I'm ready to start doing the homework that will get me there, if you don't mind being my tutor."

"I would love to tutor you, Doctor."

He was already regretting that it could last for only a night but come tomorrow the fantasy of the evening would have worn off,

Michi would be back in her white medical coat ready to present the last lecture of the series, and his mind would be back on the list of patients he would be seeing once he was back in New York. But for now, Sapporo, Japan, or New York City were simply places on a map while here, before him, was a place in time he wanted to exploit. "So, can you walk out of this banquet room, or would you like me to carry you?"

"How about you go first and I'll follow in ten minutes?"

"So, this is to be a clandestine affair?"

"Clandestine and cautious," she said. "Because we have only tonight. This is just the fantasy. Do you understand? Tonight, the fantasy. Tomorrow, the reality."

"Yes," he said, because he wasn't a greedy man. One night was all he had in him. That was the way he structured his life. "Very good rules to live by. No relationship, no tangles. That's been my motto for years." Even though he imagined one night with Michi was more than anything he'd ever hoped for. But even in the fantasy there had to be practicality. That was the story of his life. He didn't want a real involvement. It was too complicated. Hearts got broken. Someone survived while someone else did not. No, what he did, what he had, worked. A life without those involvements suited him just fine.

"Ten minutes," he said, brushing a slow, lush kiss to her lips before turning and walking away. Yes, ten minutes before his world would change, even if only for one night. But, for the first time in his life, he felt oddly uncomfortable with that arrangement. To think about why or put thought into it would only ruin the moment, and he wanted this moment like he'd wanted no other before. So, he put it out of his mind as he pushed the elevator button and went to his room on the sixth floor.

Michi stood in the hall outside his door for several minutes, simply staring. Was she totally out of her head, seducing him the way she'd just done? She paced back and forth for a little while, downed the rest of her champagne, wished she had another glassful. Then finally she drew in a deep breath, bent down and took off her ungodly uncomfortable shoes, stepped up to his door and knocked.

When he opened to her, she simply handed him her shoes on the way in, and it took a full twenty seconds before she realized he'd already rid himself of his shirt. And there he was, the perfect image of the man of her dreams. Interesting, smart, a little intense. The typical tall, dark, handsome hunk. Smoldering. Sexy. Virile. Provocative. Seductive. All those descriptions from her fantasies come to life. All hers for a little while.

"You're thinking too much," he said, as he shut the door and tossed the shoes aside.

"Good thoughts," she said.

"About me, I hope." He started to walk toward her, but Michi held out her hand to stop him.

"Playing games?" he asked.

"Making memories."

He chuckled. "We haven't done anything to make memories of, Michi, and if you've changed your mind, it's not too late for you to turn around and go back downstairs to the reception you're hosting. That would be the practical thing to do."

"Maybe I don't want practical," she said, moving closer to him, then raising her hand to slide it around his neck. "Maybe I'm always practical and tonight I want something else." Even though her mind was still a little wobbly, it was made up. One night, one time with one perfect man. The handsome stranger who would come and go in her life and leave her with a memory of the time she'd stepped outside herself to do something daring. No strings, no attachments. Throw caution to the wind this once, because the wind had never thrown anything back that wasn't painful.

So, no, it wasn't her style, but she didn't want it to be. Just once she wanted to know what being bold and reckless would feel like, as being anything else hadn't gotten her what she wanted. But one night of excitement with Eric and maybe that would be enough before she stepped back into her life and its harsh realities.

And Eric was… He was pure, raw sex and total excitement. And she wanted it all.

CHAPTER ONE

MICHI SATO LOOKED UP at the massive building, wondering how many stories high it was. She guessed somewhere between twenty-five and thirty, all belonging to Eric and, maybe someday, Riku?

She really hadn't given Eric's status much of a thought up until now, and simply seeing his name in gold looming over the massive bank of revolving glass doors caused her stomach to churn. Even as outgoing as she was, she wasn't up to this. Finding herself so close to Eric now, after all this time, caused too many unanswered questions to come to mind.

Her motivation for that night, his motivation as well. Certainly nothing long term had been meant. They'd both made that clear during pillow talk and foreplay. Then look what had happened. Especially after her doctor had told her only weeks before it was an impossibility. That her condition had gone from bad to abandon all hope.

"I'm so glad he was wrong," she said, kissing Riku on the cheek. "Mommy hasn't done everything the best way she could have, but that's all going to change now." After Eric knew he had a son. After Riku's surgery. There were so many things weighing her down now, so much guilt she had to come to terms with, she didn't know where to begin. But she was here to start a new course. At least, that was what she kept telling herself. New course, new direction, new leaf turned over. It sounded good, but in practice…well, that was the part she wasn't sure about. But the first step was behind her now, and that was good.

Of course, she'd told herself other things, too, that she'd backed away from, hadn't she? Namely, not telling Eric he was daddy to her two-year-old. She'd tried, had made futile attempts at calling, texting and using any other means of electronic communication available. Then she'd given up. But that didn't make things better. In fact, in the long run it would make things worse than she could probably even imagine.

"Mommy's going to make it all better," she said. How? She didn't know. But she'd figure it out.

And now, on the second step of her journey—trying to figure out how to tell him—here she was, looking in Eric's window, holding his son, and so confused her head was spinning. In just a few days Riku's long-awaited surgery would take place—a surgery Eric should know about as it had been his specialty when he'd been a practicing surgeon.

Of course, that would have meant telling Eric somewhere along the way that he had a son, then also telling him his son had a heart defect. Neither of which she'd done. Yet. Except the *yet* part was looming like a black raincloud over her. All the good intentions in the world wouldn't stop it from bursting and pouring down on her. It was up to her to make the plan that would avoid it—step into a doorway or, in this case, Eric's office.

But, no. Instead, here she was, like a little girl with her nose to the toy-store window, hoping for the prettiest doll inside. Expecting to get it but fearing she wouldn't. Expecting Eric to overlook that she'd kept his son from him all this time but fearing he would not forgive her. And in some fragmented way, hoping the three of them could become a family on some level. All while the black cloud was getting closer and closer to bursting.

"Be glad you're too young to know about responsibilities," she said to Riku, turning so her body would shield his from the slight gust of warm wind whipping up the streets and down the alleys. "Or how to make something right you've already made such a mess of."

Realistically, she wasn't counting on things turning out well as far as Eric was concerned. Sure, he could walk away from the entire situation, which didn't seem at all like the man she'd known for little more than a night. Or he might recognize Riku as his son, then want more of Riku in his life than she was prepared to give him. And that seemed the greater possibility. But would he go so far as try for full custody since she'd hidden his sick child from him for two years? Or argue that she was negligent given how he was an expert in the procedure his son needed to have done?

This was what scared her. And why Eric scared her. He might want more of Riku than she could bear to give up. Now, she feared, she was about to find out just how much, and she wasn't sure what she'd do once she knew. Wasn't ready for that, wasn't ready to face the consequences she'd set into motion, whatever they might be.

Still, she had always to remember this was about Riku, not her. Not even Eric. Right now, her son was the only one who counted, and when she did tell Eric about him, she hoped he would be able to see that was the case. At least until after Riku's surgery.

"Your daddy's inside that building, Riku," she said, turning again so the boy bundled in her arms could look through the window. "He's a very nice man. And kind. A perfect man to be your father. I know you don't understand what I'm telling you, but you will someday."

And she prayed he didn't hate her when he did understand, even when she'd finally gathered the courage to correct her mistakes long before Riku would be old enough to hate her for what she'd done.

That was another fear she had to live with: the possibility that Riku could turn away from her once he was old enough to know what his mother had done. If that day ever came, well…she wouldn't think about it. The way she hadn't thought about other consequences.

So, true to form, she wasn't going to deal with that now, when she was so confused, so angry at herself, and so afraid for her son's life. Especially not when every ounce of everything inside her was devoted to Riku and what was ahead for him.

"I wish you could tell me what to do," she told Riku, snuggling him in even closer to her. "Your mommy didn't make some wise choices and now she's very discouraged that what she's done might touch you in ways I never intended to happen."

Riku's response was to reach up and grab Michi's hair, then giggle.

"Do you know how cute you are?" she asked, trying to extricate herself from his playful grip. This child was her world, nothing else mattered. And it still surprised her how much she'd changed in such a short time. "OK, so you're not going to answer me. But take my word for it, you're the cutest little boy ever."

It was a mild November day, the sun was bright, the slight gusts of wind warm enough that people had taken off their jackets to enjoy the unexpected rise in temperature. But Michi tucked Riku's little fist into the blanket in which he was wrapped. So maybe she was overprotective. What of it? She'd had so much difficulty bringing him into this world.

She'd lost count of how many times she'd almost lost him before his birth; didn't know how long she'd been hospitalized to prevent a miscarriage early on and a stillbirth later. It had been such a struggle, then afterwards a beautiful baby boy…with a heart defect. All of it had been so much to deal with, the hysterectomy after Riku's birth being the least of her concerns. That mess with the social worker calling her unfit had been traumatic. So, if she wanted to be overprotective, she had good cause.

In her defense, she'd tried contacting Eric early on, but the information on him from the seminar had been old, and she'd refused to ask her aunt to forward information on to him as that would have revealed her pregnancy long before she'd wanted to. So, she'd put it off. Had promised herself she'd do it later. But later had brought her pregnancy difficulties, then a sick baby, outside complications…too many "laters" had added up until she'd known she'd passed the point of reasonability. All that, plus she simply hadn't been coping. One step at a time. That was all she had been able to manage. One difficult, often heartbreaking step at a time.

Still, she had always intended to find Eric at some point, maybe when Riku was through the worst of it. Or maybe when she wasn't so consumed by guilt and confusion and strange emotions she couldn't even identify.

Even with all the mistakes she'd made, though, look what she had. The world. Riku was the whole world to her. And now, as she hugged him and stood looking into the Hart building, the urgency to make this right was pounding at her. "He's in there somewhere," she said, hoping yet not hoping to catch a glimpse of Eric. "Anyway, it's silly standing out here, not sure what I'd do if I did see him," she said to her son. "Besides, look who's here."

She twisted so Riku could see his great-aunt walking with outstretched arms to greet them. Riku stretched his arms out to her as well.

"Just what we need," Agnes Blaine said. "A whole afternoon to spoil my nephew."

Michi laughed. "Not too much spoiling, I hope."

Takumi, Agnes's partner of twenty-five years and Michi's uncle, stepped to Agnes's side. "That would be between Riku and us."

He bent over and kissed his nephew. "And maybe the clerk in the toy store."

Michi loved these people. They'd been there for her at the end of her pregnancy, then through some of Riku's early tests. And they were part of the small circle of family she'd trusted enough to let them care for Riku for a few hours, or even a full day.

"The amount of spoiling we bestow upon our nephew is a personal matter," Agnes teased, looking up at the gold embossing over the building: *Eric Hart Property Management*. "You haven't…?"

Michi shook her head, then stepped back. Agnes and Takumi knew to leave it alone. Her whole family did. Yes, everybody knew Eric Hart was Riku's father, but it was not a topic anyone ever discussed. At least, not in front of Michi. "He's just up from his nap, so he should be good for a while. And I shouldn't be gone long." Just long enough to spend some time alone, to think.

"We'll be back home when you get there," Takumi said, pulling Michi into his arms. "Be patient with yourself," he said. "Everything will be as it's meant to be."

And, in the blink of an eye, she was alone on the sidewalk in front of Eric's building. It was the first step. And her second step would take her inside.

"No, I'm not going to my afternoon meeting. We couldn't come to terms over the phone, so I cancelled it. No point in wasting everybody's time. But Bucky Henderson is still coming in this morning since he flew all the way from Texas before I could stop him, and I'm hoping we can come to some kind of terms. I like the land he's proposing I buy, but I'm not really into what he wants to do with it. Which means I need this meeting to see if he's open to compromise."

So maybe he wasn't the best businessman in the world. Lord knew, he wasn't his old man when it came to property management and land deals, but this was his lot now. People depended on him, and he tried his best not to let them down.

"Will you need the lawyers here for the meeting?" his secretary Natalie asked.

"No. And I don't need anybody from the real estate acquisition division here either." He'd settle for it to go all his way, or even for a compromise. But if Bucky didn't buy into that... "They know what the deal is, and what I'd like to see it become, so we're set." Besides, having too many people around the business table was intimidating and while that might have been his old man's way of conducting business, it wasn't his.

"Then you've made up your mind?" Natalie asked. She was an older woman. Nearing seventy, he thought. Efficient, smart, and his dad's mistress for more than a quarter of a century. One of the many. Only Natalie was the one who'd kept him on the business track and for that devotion, no matter how misguided, Eric had let her stay, despite the badly kept secret that she'd played some part in his parents' divorce. But Natalie wasn't alone—there was the part his mother had played in the story, a part he knew nothing about.

"Not entirely. But I'm getting closer."

"Your father would have had this deal wrapped up weeks ago," Natalie reminded him. Her gray hair pulled back into a knot at the base of her neck, her glasses riding low on her nose, her perpetual frown and critical tone…there were days he wished she'd retired. Pretty much most days. But, like everything else, he felt an obligation to right his dad's wrongs. And there were so many of them. As for Natalie, she was just a drop in his father's unfortunate ocean.

"Of course he would have. But I'm not my father. I'm a surgeon, and as a surgeon I don't just hop into a procedure without knowing every angle of it." He forced a friendly smile, even though he knew Natalie would take one more shot. She always did.

"You *were* a surgeon," she reminded him. "Past tense, Eric. Remember that."

"You're right, of course. I *was* a surgeon." At heart, he still was. But circumstances had changed when his dad had died, leaving him not only an international property management corporation but a billion dollars, windmills, camels and God only knew what else.

Oh, his dad hadn't expected he'd be able to run the company and had even gone so far as to make provisions to put the governance under the control of a hand-picked board. Hand-picked by his father, of course. In other words, ten daddy clones trying to rule his life instead of one daddy. He'd fired them and put into place various people who made sense to him. An environmentalist, a construction engineer, a social worker, even a teacher. All people he respected and admired and not a designer suit amongst them.

"Look, I'm going across the street for coffee."

"But we have that expensive coffee system your father had put in."

"We have a coffee system that makes espresso, latte macchiato, cappuccino and even milk foam. It makes café mocha, *frappé* and *yungyang*, whatever the hell that is. But what it doesn't make is a decent cup of black coffee. So, I'll run out and grab one, then I'll be back in time to meet with Bucky. Oh, and if the coffee machine doesn't make anything he prefers, text me and I'll bring him a cup of black coffee, too."

"He's a busy man, Eric," she warned. "Don't keep him waiting."

He never did. A habit from his doctor days, he supposed. But Natalie always said it, and he always responded with, "I won't." While gritting his teeth. "Anyway, would you like something?" he asked. "Regular coffee, tea, a scone?"

Every time he asked she always looked surprised. Probably because his dad had never made a simple, kind gesture toward her. Which, in a way, was the same boat he was in. Always trying to find a way to get noticed by his dad, and never succeeding. So, while she may have had the occasional romp in his father's bed and a paycheck, at the end of her day she'd always gone home alone. Just like he had, until he'd been sent off to boarding school.

Was there a term that meant more than

alone? Because that was what he'd always felt growing up…more than alone. The one left out. Left behind. Forgotten. An obstacle in his dad's path.

"I'm perfectly fine with what your father's coffee system makes," she said.

Poor Natalie. Always the trouper. And always let down. Yep, he knew the feeling. "OK, then I'll be back in a few." Even though he would have preferred a nice walk, or maybe some people-watching in Central Park, he didn't have a choice. That wasn't his life now. Getting back to Bucky Henderson to discuss the purchase of a large chunk of Texas for a casino with all the frills was.

Sighing, Eric stood after Natalie left, then went to the window. His dad's office had always been at the top—the twenty-fifth floor. In a massive corner suite, with plate-glass views of the city in all directions. His own office, however, was on the second floor, one window, limited view, and small in comparison to what awaited him on the top floor. Occupying it was an egregious act, he supposed.

One that signaled ambivalence. And being at the top signified power. So, his defiant little office on the second floor would probably speak volumes to a shrink, if he cared to go that route. Which he didn't. But none of it really mattered, did it? He did his job, his employees had their lives secured, and the world kept spinning.

For a moment, Eric scrutinized the people walking on the sidewalk below. Where were they going? Why were they in such a hurry? Were they happily married or cheating on an unsuspecting spouse? He liked speculating about other people's lives since he barely had one of his own. Speculating made him feel like he was still in touch, even though he knew damn well he wasn't.

One last glance before he headed out for coffee and someone down there caught his eye. From his vantage he couldn't see much of her, so he adjusted for a better look and what he saw was well worth the effort. *She* was walking with a purpose. Long strides that outdistanced all the people around her. Shouldering her way through all the congestion like a woman with a purpose. He could almost hear the click of her heels on the cement, she was moving so fast. Like a whirlwind whooshing in and out of the crowd. And beautiful. Black hair pulled back away from her face. A stunning figure that men could only dream about.

She was Japanese, he thought. Reminded him of Michi…her height, her stature. Michi… so often on his mind. The one he shouldn't have let get away. But in the nearly three years since he'd spent that incredible night with her, too much had happened. Too many responsibilities had pulled him away from what he wanted to do and dumped him into the pile of all the things he *had* to do.

There had been a time Michi had been what he'd wanted. Maybe in some ways, she still was. But it was too late for that. He'd made his choice the morning he'd left without a goodbye. After that, there was no turning back.

Michi was the one he regretted walking away from, though. The only one. Even now, she floated through his mind in the unguarded moments, taunting him for what he'd missed out on. One night only. It was what he'd told her because it was what he'd meant. Something had happened that night. Something that had unhinged him and compelled him to do what he'd never done before—given himself over to a casual fling that had turned out to be so much more. At least, in his thoughts. Still, one night with Michi…

Eric closed his eyes, conjuring up her image. Funny how what he remembered of her seemed to meld with the woman he'd just seen on the walkway outside. Maybe it was because he'd never truly gotten over her. Granted, they'd only known each other a few hours when the text that had changed his life had come. But in those few hours…it had been like he'd known her for days, or weeks, or months. Maybe his whole life. Could she have been the one? He didn't know as he'd never found himself in that mindset before. The possibilities hadn't escaped him, however. And as she'd lain there next to him, her breath sounds so tiny and precise, he'd simply listened, and wondered what would happen if they had one more night.

Unfortunately, the opportunity to go beyond that night had never happened. Still, in the very few—as in could be counted on one hand—dates he'd had with other women since then, nothing had ever seemed right. To himself, he'd nitpicked every woman to pieces before their date, then always cut the evening short because she hadn't what he'd wanted. And for sure, he'd never dated any of those hopefuls twice. Because of his job, he always told himself. Yes, because of his job.

But somewhere in all that mess, thoughts of Michi pushed everything away. Even now, when he should be concentrating on Bucky's proposal, his mind was wandering back to Sapporo, to that one perfect night.

Which meant it was time to go get that coffee, refocus, and figure out his next step in the Texas land acquisition deal. So, Eric put on his suit coat—he really hated wearing suits every day, but that was the dress code, so he observed it—took a quick look in the mirror in his private bathroom, straightened his tie, then traced, with his left index finger, all the new lines and creases that were beginning to show. So many changes to his body in the past couple of years. *What did it matter?*

There had been a time when he'd appreciated the sideways glances of the nurses who hadn't known he knew they were watching. And that obvious flirtation from Michi in Japan…something that had twisted and turned him in ways he hadn't expected then, and even now. So maybe the looks weren't going down too badly, but what he saw staring back at him from the mirror was a man who was… resigned to something that didn't make him happy. Didn't satisfy him either. Didn't give him the good, hard feeling of being tired but satisfied that made him sleep well at night. As long as he spent his days behind this desk, doing mediocre work at best, it would always be that way.

"But we keep promising to fix things, don't we?" he always said to his mirror, ever hopeful that saying it out loud to an inanimate object that wouldn't criticize him might actually inspire him to go out and find some of that old mojo again. And did he ever need that inspiration. Where and how, though? He didn't have a clue. But at least all hope hadn't died. That was something to hang onto. Although sometimes hanging only by a thread.

Once Eric decided he was "Hart-ready," as his dad had called it, he headed for his office door. And his thoughts—on the woman he'd seen outside. The fairy-tale would have them bump into each other in the coffee shop, then spend hours talking, laughing, getting to know each other. They would make plans for dinner that night—someplace slow and dim, where they could talk quietly and tell secrets. Then they'd go back to his place…and that was where it stopped.

Those days were behind him even though he was only thirty-six, and now he was all about the corporate life where everything ran on fear and promises, and most of those promises were empty, like his social life.

"Sure you don't want something?" he asked

Natalie again, as he headed out the door. The fact that she didn't even take her eyes off her computer screen didn't surprise him. Now, as she did so often, she was looking through her gallery of pictures of the only man she'd ever loved. Lost in his world. Reliving the life she'd never had. Sad. But sometimes the choices people made weren't easily shed. For Natalie, that was his father. For him…trying to please a man who would never be pleased. And now it was too late.

Would that be him someday? Sitting at a computer, looking through reminders of a life he had never had, and an undertaking in which he'd failed so miserably. He sincerely hoped not.

CHAPTER TWO

IT WAS A cozy little café. Pastries, teas, coffee, flowers, and all sorts of gifty things that were cute, but not practical. And the café was full to overflowing with people. Loud, but nice. Michi had managed to snag the last table available, the one in the corner, the one with the worst view in the shop. But that didn't matter. She wasn't in the mood for being social or enjoying views. All she wanted was a tea, and some time by herself to think.

She was worried, naturally. Riku would be in great hands with Dr. Kapoor. She was sure of that. But right now, that wasn't her biggest concern. It was Eric, and what to do about that whole situation. He had a right to know he had a son. He also had a right to know his son had a heart defect. But hadn't she tried to contact him early on her pregnancy? Then later, after Riku was born, hadn't she tried again?

Well, that was the way she pacified herself when she got in the mood. Telling herself she'd tried. That she'd been so overwhelmed that her thinking hadn't been sharp. Sometimes it worked, sometimes it did not. Today it wasn't even coming close because her motivations were not even clear to herself anymore. Except for one. But that had nothing to do with Eric, and it was something she surely didn't want him to know: being accused of being an unfit mother.

So, there was that weight she always carried, as well as not telling Eric the truth from the start. And, of course, her default excuse... yeah, right, she'd tried. What of it?

Yet he was right across the street now. Easy, convenient. All she had to do was walk over there—and then what? Would she produce papers proving Riku was Eric's? Wait, she didn't have papers. Hadn't even put Eric's name on the birth certificate. So, would he simply believe her? *Hello, Eric. I had your baby two years ago.* Probably not. Then there was always the question of whether he'd want to be an involved father. She knew he'd be a good father, just from the little she knew of him. But would he want that?

There were so many questions with answers awaiting her. Answers she feared. So, for now, she'd sip her tea and hope for an angel or something to drop down from the sky and give her the solution she needed because she sure wasn't in any state to figure it out on her own.

"Would you care for a refill on your tea?" a young man asked, startling Michi out of her thoughts. "Another tea bag, more hot water?"

She looked up at him and smiled. "That would be lovely," she said, gazing beyond the server to the table where four women sat chattering away as they ate their pastries. "With a little more lemon," she added. "And maybe one of those scones I saw earlier when I was at the counter."

"Happy to oblige, ma'am," the young man said, then scooted through the tangle of people who weren't lucky enough to have a place to sit but who obviously weren't ready to go back outside and face the rest of the day.

Michi leaned back in her chair, trying to relax, but she was too wound up for that, so she simply sipped her tea, ate her scone when the server brought it, and stared out the window at Eric's building, like that was going to give her some kind of resolution. Intermittently, she flipped through her phone to various photos of Riku and only then did that feeling of despair go away. One perfect little face with such a calming effect. Who would have ever guessed that she could have fallen in love so deeply. But she had, and she would literally give her life for that little boy.

"I hope you like blueberry, because I've bagged up one to take with you. You look like you're in a blueberry kind of mood," the server said, handing over a bag. "On the house."

"Thank you," she said, as she repositioned herself in the seat. "So, tell me—what, exactly, identifies a blueberry mood?"

"Someone who's worrying or being contemplative. You've been in here quite a while and it's obvious something's on your mind. Something heavy, judging from all the frowning."

Was she so transparent that the young man with the scones could identify her mood? He was right—it was definitely blueberry. "Maybe if I come back, I'll be in a strawberry mood. Would that be better?"

"Yes, because our strawberry scones are one of the most popular and strawberry is a very happy state of mind."

"Then make sure you save me a strawberry and I'll work hard on my strawberry mood before I get here." She took a bite of her blueberry scone, then a sip of her tea, and started to pop back into her photo gallery, but a voice at a nearby table startled her out of her plan.

"Help! Somebody, please, help. She's choking."

Instantly alert, Michi jumped up and ran to the table where the ladies she'd observed were sitting. Sure enough, one of them was choking. Sitting up straight, confused, trying to breathe, the woman rolled her eyes up at Michi, and her expression was beyond frightened. She was dying, and she knew it.

"Please, stand back," Michi yelled to the crowd, as she leaned the choking woman forward and slapped her back five times. She'd hoped that whatever was lodged in the woman's windpipe would come loose, but unfortunately that didn't happen.

So, from behind again, she wrapped her arms around the woman's ribcage, forming a fist with both hands. Then she pulled the woman toward her, giving an upward thrust each of the five times she tried. Still, nothing happened. And now the woman was turning blue. Her lips, her fingernails. Oxygen deprivation, Michi knew as she started the whole procedure over again. "Has somebody called for an ambulance?" she shouted to the crowd.

One deep, smooth voice stood out over the noise of the crowd. "ETA less than five," he said, pushing himself through the crowd, then kneeling next to Michi. "And she doesn't have five minutes left in her," he continued.

Michi looked over to see who was working with her, and gasped. "Eric?"

"Michi?" he said, as he took over the upward thrusts Michi was doing. One, two—on the third thrust it worked and the woman sucked in a deep breath.

"Stay still," Michi cautioned her, trying not to think what would happen next, when the ambulance took her to the hospital. "The paramedics will be here shortly, and they'll take you to the emergency room so the doctors there can run some tests to make sure you're good."

Gasping for breath, the woman nodded her understanding as Eric took her pulse again. "Much better," he said, giving her a reassuring pat on the arm. "You've come through the hard part like a champ, and this next part in the hospital will be much easier. And it won't be happening on a cold cement floor."

She smiled up at him, drew in a deep breath, then closed her eyes, not from fear but from trusting Eric, who'd taken off his jacket and placed it under her head.

The way Eric was with the poor woman…it nearly brought a lump to Michi's throat. This was a man who was born to be a doctor. A man who shouldn't have given it up. And he was Riku's father, she thought as a swell of pride overtook her. "Paramedics are on their way in," she said, glancing out the window, not so much to watch for the paramedics as to pull herself together.

Immediately, the onlookers in the café began to move tables and chairs back and push the display shelf of coffees and mugs for sale to the wall to make room for the two paramedics, their equipment and their stretcher. "Her vitals are stabilizing," Eric said. "So now it's more about her being frightened than anything else."

The woman looked up at him again and nodded, and Michi was still amazed by the way not only the woman but everyone in the room responded to him. Even in the middle of a medical crisis his voice was so calm, so reassuring she was impressed by how much she remembered the detail of it. It was the same deep, convincing undertone that had seduced her. The same richness that had enticed her into his bed. Yet now she could hear the edge, the command. And she could see the way people were responding.

"I was actually thinking about you earlier," Eric said.

There hadn't been a day gone by since he'd left her that she hadn't thought about him. She'd sculpted the perfect words to say when she did finally catch up to him. Practiced them. Edited. Practiced. Edited. And now that the moment had arrived, all she could think to say was, "How have you been?" Stupid. Stupid. And she didn't hear his answer between the noise of people still moving tables back and the mad flurry of the pounding feet of people trying to get out of the way.

"She's doing better," Michi said, as Eric bent down again, but this time not as keen to watch the patient as he was to look at her. "Respirations still shallow and fast, but nothing dangerous."

Ruth, the choking victim, smiled at Eric like

he was the only one in the room as the paramedics took quick vital signs, then lifted her onto the stretcher. At that point, Eric took her hand and went with them to the ambulance, and it was only when they had arranged her in the back and were getting ready to shut the door that he let go. Once he did, he slapped the door to indicate everything was good, and the ambulance siren came on, then the vehicle nosed its way into bumper-to-bumper New York traffic.

"She really trusted you," Michi said, standing behind him.

"I think if you're in a life or death situation and there's somebody there to help you, you naturally trust them. Haven't been in one myself, but it makes sense."

"How have you been, Eric?" she asked again as they walked back over to the sidewalk.

"Busy. New responsibilities, a new job, a new life."

"Medicine's loss," she said, clearly uneasy. This wasn't the right place to tell him about Riku, neither was it the right time. But it was circling around her now, the reality of what she was about to face. "My, um…aunt mentioned you'd left surgery to take over your family business."

"Duty called," he said. "But that's life, right? Things happening when you least expect it. Like you. I thought I saw you outside my building a while ago," he said, following her back through the congestion of people and displaced tables and chairs in the café. "Standing on the sidewalk."

"I was taking a walk earlier, so you might have." Since he wasn't mentioning the baby she'd been carrying, she assumed he hadn't seen Riku. "I was on my way to order coffee and a scone," she answered, then laughed. "Which is pretty obvious since we met in a shop where they sell coffee and scones."

"Good coffee, great scones. So, can I get you something? The blueberry scones are the best, in my opinion."

Blueberry. That caused her to laugh. Today she must have simply reminded everybody of a blueberry, and that one little scone held so many ramifications, her stomach turned over and all she wanted was to turn around and get out of there, blueberry scone or not. "After what just happened, I'm out of the mood," she said.

"Well, I've got a secretary back in the office who's expecting delivery service, even though she'll deny it, so..." He stepped on ahead to the counter, placed his order, then turned back to Michi, who'd taken several steps toward the door. "Not that it's any of my business but are you in New York for any reason in particular?"

To find him? No. To find herself, perhaps. Mostly, though, for Riku. "Family," she said. "My uncle and his partner are here, and..." She shrugged as she took another couple of steps backward toward the door. Opened it, then hesitated for a moment. "Look, I need to get going. They're expecting me."

"I wish I'd known you were coming. Maybe we could have set aside an evening..."

"Maybe," she said on a wistful sigh as she stepped out onto the sidewalk.

"Is it too late for that? Since I'm the boss I

can juggle my schedule. Maybe something to-night? Dinner?"

That could be the perfect time and place to tell him everything. Which was why she was hesitating. Her fear of what she had to do was finally turning into her reality. "It's not like we started anything real that night. Then the way you left me... I mean, I didn't have expectations. But when you do what we did, I should think there'd be a civil goodbye at the end of it." Except failed contraception had turned that into an impossibility because she had Riku now. And no regrets, except her actions.

But if she did decide to tell Eric, would he have regrets? Well, now wasn't the time to tell him, and now wasn't the time to discover the answer to her question. Maybe that angel had dropped down when she wasn't looking and left her with enough of a solution to get her by for a little while. But only for a little while as she still felt unsettled. "Seven," she finally said. "At my uncle's restaurant." A comfort zone she desperately needed now.

"Which is?"

"Tanoshī Shō, if you don't mind eating Japanese food. It's small, quiet, and the chef… they don't come any better than Takumi. But if you'd prefer a steak, or something Italian…"

"What I'd prefer is an hour or two of your time, Michi. That morning when I left…it never felt resolved. You know, lacking the whole closure thing people talk about today."

"Waking up alone in bed is closure enough," she said, even though she felt the same way he did.

"Then bear with me. There are some things I need to tell you, for my sake."

"You left me," she said, slinging her purse over her shoulder. "We weren't…aren't…anything, and we knew what we were about, so what happened happened."

"I had a good reason."

"And the author Jean Renoir once said, *'The truly terrible thing is that everybody has their reasons.'*" She didn't want to be obstinate, didn't want to sound so harsh or rejecting since she too had her reasons. But this was fear bubbling up in her. Pure, raw fear. Everything that had scared her these past nearly three years was finally confronting her, and she had to get it right or too many people would be hurt.

"Look, I don't want to get into this here. I've got a meeting in a few minutes so tonight…"

Michi swallowed hard, then nodded. "Tonight," she repeated, then managed a smile. "But only if you try my uncle's peanut *amanattō*."

"I don't believe I know that one," Eric replied.

"He doesn't make it for the general public. Mostly for his family." And in a way Eric was family. "Here, in America, his desserts are a little more Western, but back home this was always a real treat. In fact, there's a version without the peanuts that Riku loves…" She caught herself before she said anything else. This wasn't the way to tell him. Not here. Not now. Not a casual mention in a going-nowhere conversation.

"Riku?" Eric questioned. "Who's Riku?"

"I'll meet you there at seven," she said, then scooted around him and headed down the sidewalk, not sure where she was going.

But any place away from Eric was good. He'd had such a profound effect on her the first time they'd met that within the first hours she had wondered if their meeting could be the start of something more. Not expecting Riku to be the something more, of course. But everything about Eric was potent and powerful, which was everything she'd needed that night. Someone to push out the reality and offer the fantasy.

And look at her now. All about the reality, and nothing else. But as she thought every time she looked at her son, *No regrets*. Her medical practice was nearly a thing of the past now, she spent more time in doctors' offices and doing online research than she'd ever imagined could happen in her life. Every waking minute was fixed on Riku and the next thing she needed to do for him, whether it was bathing him or feeding him, adjusting his oxygen when he required it, or simply cuddle time.

Definitely no regrets, though. Only love for Riku, and maybe a little bit left over for the man who had given her Riku. Because, after all, without knowing it, Eric had redefined her life, given her a purpose far greater than anything she'd ever known. For that, her soft spot for him was large. Larger than she could have ever imagined.

CHAPTER THREE

MICHI WALKED WITH a purpose. He'd noticed that when he'd seen her on the sidewalk below and hadn't known who she was. It was that walk that had captured him. Maybe because it had been familiar? Maybe because he'd remembered it so keenly from the first time they'd met, then tucked it away as part of a memory of a night he'd wanted to go so right yet had gone so wrong.

So, she was here to visit family. Agnes and her husband, he presumed. But she'd also mentioned someone called Riku and for a moment he fixed on that. Maybe a little jealously, even though he didn't have that right. So, who was this Riku? Was he a friend or lover? Maybe a husband? He'd asked, but she'd avoided answering. Did she wear a wedding ring now?

Or even an engagement ring? Why hadn't he looked?

Michi married? That was an idea he didn't want to consider, maybe because somewhere in the middle of their one night, he'd caught himself wondering if that had the potential to turn into something more. She'd simply seemed to…fit, and he'd even caught himself planning some quick trips to Sapporo every now and then. Maybe he'd find a way to bring some of his business there, to give him the excuse to visit. Or he'd simply be direct and tell Michi he wanted to see if they could have more. Take her to that secluded little cabin in the mountains his father had owned, let her best him at skiing, even though he was pretty darned good.

Hot chocolate by the fireplace during the winter. A walk through the stunning Onze Harukayama Lily Garden in the summer. A trip by rope car up Mount Moiwa in the autumn to enjoy the stunning panoramic view of Sapporo's turning colors.

But then his dad had died, and Eric had had

to make an emergency trip back home. Corporate jet waiting, he'd been out of the hotel room and out of Michi's life ten minutes after the notification. He'd tried texting, but it had bounced back. Had tried calling, but even in this modern age of technology, that hadn't worked either. Then life had gotten so complicated, and his struggle to keep up with it had turned into an almost never-ending battle.

Unfortunately, Michi had been lost in all that, and by the time his life had settled down enough to get back in touch with her, which was what he'd wanted to do, it had been a year and a half later. Too much time had gone by and he'd been headed in an entirely different direction—one that would never work for Michi as she was so devoted to her practice. So why try to start something with her when he was barely keeping his head above water?

Even though he'd thought about her off and on all that time, it had been easier to shut the door on all possibilities—or as some would call them, hopes and dreams—and move on. As they said, timing was everything, and his was off in the worst kind of way. "Well, you're stuck with this life now," he said to himself on his way back to his desk. "No point in worrying."

Bucky was waiting for him when he got back. Actually pacing the floor like a caged tiger, which put Eric instantly on alert. Nervous people made him nervous. That was something new, as he'd expected nervousness when he'd been a surgeon. But nervousness in business worried him, because to Eric it always meant the worrier knew something he didn't, and that was a bad place to be when you were in the middle of a business deal. "So, how's it been going?" he asked, as Bucky took the seat across the desk from Eric.

"Good," Bucky said, then repeated himself. "Good."

"And I'm assuming you want an answer from me today?"

"Moving along with this deal would be to everyone's advantage," he said. "Money-wise, this is our best chance. If we hesitate any longer, we'll either lose the property altogether or the cost of it will go up."

That sounded just like his father, always answering with a warning and a dire consequence. *If you don't take over the company someday, Eric, do you know how many lives will be changed, and not for the good?* That was one he'd started hearing when he wasn't even ten.

Then there was always the classic, *When you interrupt me like this, it costs money. Losing money may mean losing jobs. Losing jobs means people get hurt. Is that what you want to happen?* In other words, go away, little boy.

But the one that stood out most in Eric's mind was when his father would force him to make a choice, then ridicule him for it. *Are you sure that's what you want, Eric? Have you thought it through? Looked at consequences on both sides? Because from what I'm observing you've made a very poor choice. It's not worthy of you, and what you do reflects on me.*

That had been the day his dad had put warehouse specs and details in front of him and told him to read everything very carefully as the decision whether or not to buy was totally up to him. He'd been eleven and he'd chosen not to buy for what he'd believed were sound reasons: bad location, too old, not accessible enough. His dad had reversed his decision, though, gone ahead and purchased the structure, then lost a ton of money. For years he'd blamed it on Eric for not standing behind his convictions. "You'll never be a good businessman," he'd said.

Well, his dad had been right. He wasn't. At least, not in the way his dad would have wanted.

"I'm going to be honest with you, Bucky. I don't want to be part of the deal as it stands."

Bucky stopped dead in his tracks then stood and stared at Eric. "Seriously? We've been waiting far longer than we should have and after it all, you say no?"

"It's not a good fit." He really didn't want to have this argument, not with Michi taking over all his thoughts now, and he'd hoped that once he'd stated his decision he could simply move on. But Bucky looked like he was gearing up for a fight. His ruddy face was turning redder, his breathing was getting shallow.

"Sorry to disappoint you, but right now I'm looking more at investing in a chain of low-cost medical clinics, and I don't want to get tied up in too many new ventures at once. Unless..." He slid an offer across the desk to Bucky. One that set aside half the acreage for a wildlife habitat. Bucky took one look, then crumpled the paper and threw it in the trash.

"Seriously, Eric? A wildlife habitat on property that valuable? What would your daddy say?"

Eric didn't have to guess. He already knew. "He'd pull it out of my hands and take it over for himself."

"And you're set to go against that?"

"He's dead, Bucky. The company is mine now, and I like wildlife habitats and low-cost medical clinics."

"They're nice, but at what cost? Because they suck money, Eric. They don't make it."

It's not always about making money," Eric

defended, ready for this conversation to end and for Bucky to go away. "Sometimes you just have to do the right thing." This was the way it always happened when he didn't do what people expected, just because it was what his dad would have done. The comparisons were always harsh. People made it clear they didn't respect him or his decisions. But none of this was new to him. People had started the accusations when he was young. He'd grown up with the comparisons. He'd gotten used to the ridicule.

Still, sometimes he did wonder what would happen if he did what his dad would have done. Then he'd chalk it up to a lifetime of attempted and failed Daddy-pleasing and move on. Because in the end it didn't matter. His dad hadn't given him credit for anything, ever. Not when the old man had been alive. And now that he was dead…who the hell cared? Still, sometimes old habits squirmed their way back in. But not this deal. Not anymore.

"Your daddy wouldn't have liked this. Not one little bit. He was a smart man who knew how to take almost any property and turn it into a gold mine. Except wildlife preserves and low-cost health clinics. We both know what he would have said about those."

Ah, yes. This was his dad come back to haunt him in the guise of a slick Texas attorney. "I looked at the land, Bucky. Saw how many ranchers we'd have to displace. It was never mentioned in any of the paperwork, but there are nineteen active ranches out there. Nineteen livelihoods. Nineteen people depending on that land."

"But they'll leave when we offer them a fair price, Eric. Everybody has a price, you know. Besides, it's good land. Just far enough away from everything that when people come to the casino they'll probably stay a day or two. And it's close enough to the population base that it won't be too inconvenient. Meaning lots of cash flow. *Cha-ching.*" He gestured as if he was pulling the handle of a slot machine.

This got down to the fundamental difference between his dad and him. His dad's profit had been meant to line his dad's pockets. The profit Eric made went to something different, something better, in his opinion. Buildings and property management were necessary, but so were humanitarian efforts and charities and people in general. And coyotes. He thought about the little coyote pup he'd seen on that land, and wondered what would happen to all the displaced species, both animal and plant life. Would they just be plowed under and forgotten? That thought, more than anything, was the deciding factor. So was Bucky's attitude, to be honest.

"So your intention is to move in, bulldoze everything under and shove aside the lives that get in your way, then build your own version of paradise by the light of a slot machine?"

"Not shove, Eric. Convince. We'll convince them to move on."

"And start over, like it or not."

"Has to be done. Some of those ranches are in the path of progress so they become part of the deal."

"Maybe you think it has to be done, but not by me. That's not the kind of deal to which I want to attach the Hart name." No, his deal was to favor the coyotes and the prickly pear cactus and the ranchers. Preserving posterity, even if that posterity was not his own. The older he got, the more he thought about it.

"Is there anything I can say or do to help you change your mind? Up your percentage of the deal. Build you a custom suite in the complex with everything you could ever want in it? Introduce you to my sister...for God's sake, Eric. Be reasonable here."

"I am being reasonable." It was a sound decision. Possibly the best one he'd made since taking over the company, and he felt good about it. Somehow he thought Michi would approve, and that made him feel even better. Of course, it wasn't the same feeling he'd had when he'd left the operating theater after a good surgery, but in his line of work now it was probably as close as he would get. "I appreciate the opportunity, but it's not for me."

Bucky nodded, but ignored the hand Eric extended to him. "Your daddy wouldn't have missed this opportunity. He was an astute man who knew a good deal when it was presented to him and he always jumped right on it."

"If he were here, I'm sure he'd be flattered by the compliment. But I'm the one who's here now, making the decisions. Not my dad." And for the first time since he'd taken over, he felt like he was on solid footing. Maybe because seeing Michi again had sparked a little optimism he'd been lacking since he'd left medicine. Or maybe he was simply coming into his own. Whatever the case, this time he wasn't living in his dad's shadow, doing what his dad would have done. This was what *he* wanted, and it felt good.

"Your loss." Those were Bucky's final words before he left.

But, it wasn't a loss. Not even close to one. And Eric simply smiled as he sat back down, pulled out his cellphone, and punched in a number. "You know that piece of property down in Texas? The one they want to turn into a casino oasis? Buy it. Every last inch of it." He listened to the voice on the other end— one of his lawyers. "Yes, I'm aware of the cost.

And, no, I don't intend on selling it back to the casino investors at an inflated price. I want the land to remain as it is. I want the people who live on that land to go on living there, with the legal understanding that if they should move, that property will revert to Hart Properties. Oh, and the purpose of that property is to remain a natural habitat. Tie it up so tight that it won't be touched forever. And erect a plaque dedicating it to the coyotes."

On that positive note, and so full of positive energy he felt like he was going to burst, Eric changed out of his suit, bade Natalie good afternoon, exited the building, then took a run down to the park. It was the first time he'd run since he couldn't remember when, and it felt good. Everything felt good. Sure, Michi was a big part of that, but with this Riku somewhere in her life...well, he didn't expect anything to come of him and her. But right now he felt great, and he wasn't going to worry beyond that. He'd made a wise decision, he'd seen Michi again...so far it was turning into a very good day.

* * *

"He's had a good day," Agnes said, handing Riku over to Michi. He was sound asleep, sucking his thumb, looking as angelic as a child could look. "Although I will say he tires a little too easily, which is a concern. But..." Agnes shrugged "...Dr. Kapoor will fix him and all of us can finally breathe a sigh of relief."

"Can you watch him for a little while tonight?"

Agnes arched curious eyebrows but didn't ask.

"OK, I have a date with Eric. I ran into him and—"

Agnes raised her hand to stop her. "Your business, Michi. Entirely your business. Of course I'll watch him. Spending time with Riku is the best part of my life, except for spending time with your uncle."

"I usually put him on a little oxygen at night. That's when he seems to have the most difficulty breathing."

"And we're set up for that. Nothing to worry about."

She loved her aunt's cheery outlook, wished she had some of that herself. Maybe in time. After the surgery. After Riku was on the road to recovery.

After…after…after. That was her life. Everything now came after. But truncus arteriosus, a rare type of heart defect, pushed everything in her life aside. All she had to cling to was *after*. Everything else was a wait-and-see game.

"But I worry anyway," Michi said as she looked down at her sleeping son and tears welled in her eyes. "There are so many questions, Agnes. Should I have had this done earlier, before he was as compromised as he is now? Should I have tried harder to tell Eric when I found out? Maybe seek out his advice? Should I tell him now and leave out the part that Riku's his son? Or should I tell him everything and hope he doesn't retaliate in some way? Because that's what scares me. Would

Eric see me as negligent for my choices and go for custody?"

Agnes gave Michi's arm a squeeze. "I know you're still suffering from that incident with the social worker, but she's not Eric and I don't believe he's a vindictive man, Michi. I know him, not very well on a personal level, but what I know about him as a doctor makes me feel confident that Eric will do the right thing after *you* do the right thing."

"Which is tell him."

Agnes shrugged again, then gave her niece a bracing hug. "Have a nice time. And if you want to check on Riku, we'll do a video call."

Agnes's cheerful exterior was only for show. She was every bit as frightened as the rest of Michi's family. Still, with so much concern and support, the guilt Michi carried around was getting heavier because her common sense was right. Eric had to know. Her heart was telling her the very same thing. But it was fear holding her back, and it was a feeling she couldn't carry forever. The burden of it was too massive.

Yet when she thought of Eric's new world, that was where all her debates with herself wavered. Eric lived in a world she didn't understand now. Would Riku fit in there? Would Eric want him to fit in? She didn't know, but that wasn't going to stop her. Not now. After tonight, nothing in her world would ever be the same again. What that world was going to be, though…she wasn't ready to think about that.

Michi spent the next couple of hours sitting at the side of the bed Agnes and Takumi had placed in the spare room, simply watching Riku sleep. She loved doing that. Tried hard to do that as much as she could every day then, at the end of it when she tucked him in for the night, she kept her vigil long into the night.

Life worked out well despite her busy schedule. She saw very few patients now. Someone else had taken over the majority of her admin work. And her grandmother, a retired pediatrician, took care of Riku when Michi couldn't. Her parents were always on hand as well. So far, she'd never gone outside the family to find someone to care for Riku when she couldn't because her eager family always jumped in first.

She was lucky having so many people who cared. But Eric—did he have anyone? She didn't really know. She should, because Eric's family would also be Riku's family. Surprisingly, this was the first time she'd ever thought of that. Probably because she'd never allowed herself to accept the fact that Eric was a real part of Riku's life.

"Your daddy's a good man," she said, as Riku slowly opened his eyes. "And he won't understand a word you're saying when you start to talk because you'll speak in Japanese and he won't. Which means we may have to teach Daddy to speak our language." Riku didn't say anything, the way he never did, but he did smile, then reach up for her.

"Are you hungry?" she asked him.

Again, he didn't answer, but she always hoped. Just one word would have sent her over the moon with joy. The doctors had told her not to worry because his delay in talking was probably a side effect of his illness. Not in a medical sense, though, but more from having spent most of his life having medical treatment, which had slowed down his development in both speech and physical co-ordination. He did understand her, though. Of that, she was sure, because she could see the look in his eyes when she talked to him. "Uncle Takumi made you some applesauce. Does that sound good?"

Riku sat up and scooted toward the edge of his crib. Once there, he pulled himself to his feet, but it was difficult. He knew what to do, but his body didn't always allow it to happen. But Riku was a fighter. He struggled through, and Michi was so proud of him for that. Her son had a strong will, which would help him with some of the adaptations he'd have to make due to his heart.

"Here, let me help," she said, picking him up and putting him on her hip. "You're getting so big it's hard for Mommy to carry you." Despite his illness, he was big for his age. Was that something he'd inherited from Eric? Eric was tall, broad-shouldered, strong. She'd always known Riku might grow up to be just like his daddy. Maybe even hoped for it. And sometimes she did see Eric in him. In his smile, in the way he observed everything around him. At times she could almost see the two of them together, father and son, so alike yet so different. Her heart warmed when she fantasized them as a family. But afterwards, when her reality returned, along with it came an ache she couldn't describe because that was when she realized that not only did Eric need Riku, Riku needed Eric. And she'd let them both down.

"So, how about we get you something to eat, then we can play some games?" Then she'd go next door to meet his father and hopefully, sometime in the span of these next two hours, figure out a way to make things right for everyone. If that could happen at all.

"This is nice," Eric said, sliding into the booth alongside her. "It's one of my favorite places to eat. And it's kind of a small world, your uncle owning it."

"If you like Japanese food, this is the place to eat."

"And just like that the fantasy vanishes."

"What do you mean?" she asked.

"It was nice thinking that somehow in this vast universe we were meant to meet again."

Of course, their meeting was no coincidence, but she wasn't ready to admit that. Not yet. "Nice dream, except I'm more rooted in reality."

"Like I said, the fantasy vanishes."

"Do you really believe in fantasies coming true?" she asked him.

"I like to think they do. Haven't really had any proof to back it up, but when I was a surgeon I did witness miracles every day. And fantasies, miracles and wishes are pretty much the same thing. So, what about you? Why so... practical?"

"Because maybe a miracle happens from time to time, or maybe it's not a miracle as much as a statistic, or odds for or against you." She'd seen enough of both to be skeptical. Yet Riku was a miracle. She was firmly convinced of that even though she was skeptical of miracles otherwise. But why was she skeptical? Maybe she'd been let down too many times.

"That's too bad. My dad was like that. The only things he believed in were what he created from a practical perspective. At least, practical to him."

"But isn't what you're doing now based on practicality?"

"I bought two hundred and fifty thousand acres of desert land this morning to preserve a coyote habitat. It was slated to be a casino, but my concern was where that poor coyote would go once it was forced out of its habitat. And in my father's world there's nothing practical about that."

"What about your world, Eric?"

"It makes sense. Not practical sense, but emotional sense."

"Then you did a good thing, if you're happy with the decision."

He chuckled. "That's not what my advisors are saying. As we speak, they're probably trying to find a way to have me committed to a home for the pathetically sentimental." He scooted just a few inches closer to Michi. Not so close that he was actually touching her but close enough he felt connected, and if anyone looked on, they would assume a connection.

"Why did you leave medicine?" she asked him, as the waiter placed menus on the table. "I mean, I heard that you'd inherited a company, but when you're so good at what you do, the way you were, why give it up unless you've lost your heart for it? And judging from what I came to know at the conference, you weren't the type to lose heart for what you do...*did*."

"It's complicated," he said. "Something to do with family expectations and living up to the stature of a man I didn't particularly care to live up to. Also, I think I got myself caught up in something that was always meant to get me caught up. My dad wanted his progeny to take over where he left off, and in one way or another he prepared me for this my entire life."

"And you like it?"

"I don't dislike it the way I did at first. The

people I work with are good. I'm able to do things I could have never done before."

"Like your wildlife habitat?"

"That, and low-cost medical clinics. I fund various causes—women's health care, several sources devoted to finding cures for cardiac disease, especially in pediatrics. It all works out."

"Then you're happy?"

"I have what I need. To most people that would be happiness, I suppose."

Yet she saw such sadness in his eyes. Sadness and longing. "You're right. It does sound complicated. Do you think you'll ever return to surgery?"

"That's the question I ask myself every day as I put on my custom-tailored, five-thousand-dollar suit and wait for a limo to come pick me up for work."

"Am I detecting some cynicism?"

"More like ambivalence. Sometimes in life you end up doing what you have to do even though it's not what you want to do. I have hundreds of people in my care now who deserve to have the confidence of knowing that when they wake up tomorrow, they'll still have a job, and that they can expect pay raises and excellent working conditions. I sponsor scholarships that put their kids through college and pay for medical benefits that no other company the size of mine can come close to.

"So, while this isn't what I'd originally intended for my life, events and circumstances bring about changes we can't anticipate. What we do with those changes defines us." He stopped and took a breath. "So, how about you? Is your clinic growing the way you'd expected it to?"

"I've had some changes myself," she said, knowing this was about to become her now-or-never moment. Surprisingly, she wasn't as nervous about it as she'd expected. Something about Eric put her at ease.

"Unexpected ones?"

"Definitely unexpected. But good, because they've taught me to refocus on what's really important. Before when we…well, when we were together for that night, I didn't know what I was about. You were attractive and I wanted you…so I seduced you."

"And you did a damn fine job of it."

"But it was a diversion, Eric. An emotional response that didn't know which emotion to attach itself to."

"Then what you're telling me is that I was a practicality?"

Michi shook her head. "No. You were a re-action. I'd always wanted children, and I'd just been told that wasn't possible, given the severity of my polycystic ovarian syndrome. I was…floundering. Trying to find something to give me some stability. Something that made some sense, even if only for little while, because, trust me, one-night stands are not my normal reaction. But you were so…kind. And I felt so comfortable around you.

"So, I thought that with you I could just have one night that made sense at a time when I was drowning in a whole sea of other things that were making no sense at all. In my twenties, there was plenty of time to start a family. In my thirties, I was stripped of all my options. When we met I just wasn't coping."

It was a lot to divulge, considering no one knew any of this. Not even her family. But these were the things Eric needed to know. Things that might help him understand better.

He reached over and took her hand. "For what it's worth, I don't think I zeroed in on your vulnerability as much as your sadness. And I understand what sadness can do to a person. I'd seen it in the parents of my patients, even in myself. I wouldn't have taken advantage of you, Michi, if I'd known what you were going through."

"Well, I'm not very good at putting a lot of myself out there for other people to see. No particular reason other than that's who I am. So, what we did…it was what I wanted. Connection. Arms around me. Someone who would make me feel that I wasn't such a failure. And, yes, even though it was just for a few hours. But, other than great sex, which was my escape for a while, that night changed me, Eric. You changed me in ways I never expected could happen. Changes that couldn't happen to the woman who felt like she was failing at all the things that meant the most to her."

"And now?"

He let go of her hand and instead put his arm around her shoulder, and even in that innocent gesture, she understood how Eric had gotten to her in a way no man had ever done before. With him she felt safe. Even a bit optimistic, although that optimism might be short-lived. "Let's just say that work hasn't come first for a very long time, and it never will again. There are more important things, things that shouldn't or couldn't have happened but did."

"You've got my head spinning, Michi, because I don't understand what you're talking about." But it was serious. He could see it in the way her fists were clenched on the tabletop, and the way she avoided looking at him. Was she going to tell him she'd fallen in love that night? That would be nice, because in so many ways, so had he. Except he'd been the one to put it aside for his work, while Michi had stepped away from her work to embrace it, or something like it.

"Sometimes I don't either, Eric. And what I've done…" She took a deep breath. "I've hurt people."

"That's not possible. That's not who you are."

"But it's who I've become."

"Because of me?" he asked.

"Because of me." She twisted sideways and finally looked him straight in the eyes. "I had a baby, Eric."

He blinked, and opened his mouth to speak but closed it again.

"Despite my diagnosis, I had a baby. His name is Riku and he's changed everything in my life."

"Then you're married?" He swallowed hard as he withdrew his arm from her shoulder, pushed himself away from her, then finally braved a look at her hands to check for her wedding ring. But there wasn't one.

"No," she said, almost too quickly. "I'm a single mom."

"If this is what you want, then I should congratulate you. Especially since you didn't think it could happen."

"Don't congratulate me yet. Especially after what I've got to tell you."

A hard knot formed in his stomach. Life had certainly thrown him some curve balls, but... "How old, exactly, is Riku?"

"He's just a few weeks past his second birth-day."

"Then that night..." Even he could hear the wobble in his voice with that question.

Michi nodded. "Riku."

"And you didn't tell me?"

"It's complicated, Eric. I always intended to, and even tried to, but other things got in the way."

Right now, he was too stunned to be angry, but he knew that was coming. Could feel it bubbling up inside him. "What things were more important than telling me about my son, Michi?" The boiling anger was rising higher and higher.

"First, there was my pregnancy. It was..." As

a passing the server pushed through the door to the kitchen, and for that instant the door was wide open, Michi saw Agnes in there, holding Riku. And Riku looked limp.

A mother's instinct took over, and with no thought about Eric she bolted out of the booth and into the back room. "What's wrong?" she gasped, taking her son out of Agnes's arms.

"Fever, Michi. Too high. It came up quickly, and I was asking Takumi to drive us to the hospital."

"Who needs the hospital?" Eric asked, coming through the door. Immediately, he saw the child in Michi's arms and knew it was his son. "What's his temperature?" he demanded.

"It's one-oh-four," Agnes said, looking at Michi. "And he's beginning to sound congested, so I put him back on his oxygen and upped it a little higher than usual."

"I told him," Michi said as Eric moved to lay his hand on Riku's forehead. Tears streamed down her face as he took Riku into his arms and ran from the restaurant, holding onto his son for dear life.

Running was faster than driving or calling an ambulance, and in those few minutes, when he didn't wait for Michi to catch up, he cursed the world and the universe and Michi for keeping this secret. And even then the anger hadn't boiled up as much as he knew it still would. Why? Because he had a son who needed him. A son he had fallen in love with at first sight. A son who made him feel every bit the father he'd never expected to be.

"We're going to get you taken care of, Riku," he said as he burst through the emergency room doors and ran straight to the area sectioned off for pediatrics. "Your father will make sure you're taken care of."

"This is my son," he said to the attending who came to put Riku into one of the emergency beds. "Take good care of him." His son, he thought as the doctor carried Riku away. He had a son. And he was a father.

Eric turned as Michi caught up to him, and he saw the tears streaming down her face. Now wasn't the time, he realized. Their son was sick and that stopped everything else in the world. Now he understood what Michi had meant when she'd told him there were things more important than her medical practice. Because now, in his world, there was nothing more important than Riku.

"They'll take good care of him," he said, slipping his hand around her waist and pulling her into him. She needed his support as much as he needed hers right now, because their son was sick. *Their son...*

But soon, very soon, the inevitable reaction would happen. The anger. The frustration. The hurt. All of it. Because yet another person in his life had manipulated him. And it was Michi. The last person he'd ever thought would do that.

Maybe that, above all else, would be the biggest hurt.

CHAPTER FOUR

HOURS SEEMED LIKE DAYS, and she hadn't been allowed in to see Riku yet. They were still testing him. So, in the waiting room, Michi paced one way while Eric paced another, neither of them speaking. Eric not asking any questions because his anger was as obvious as his fear. And she was offering no explanations or apologies as right now they would fall on deaf ears, and she really needed Eric to hear her. But they were there together and, for the moment, that was the best either of them could do.

It was only after one of the nurses reassured them that Riku was stable but still had another hour of tests ahead that Michi and Eric both decided to go to the cafeteria for a break. As they were standing in line, he to pay for his coffee, she to pay for her tea, she finally broke the silence. "Don't you want to say something? Or ask me any questions?"

He turned to face her. Kept his voice low. Kept the anger on his face in check. "Other than knowing you hid my son from me, what else is there to ask? If I asked why, would you tell me? If I asked if you're sure he's mine, would you try to hide another truth from me?"

"He's yours," she said. "There hasn't been anybody else since we..."

"Great," he said, fishing a couple of bills from his pocket to pay for his coffee, then another couple to cover her tea. "You're capable of telling the truth, if that's what you just told me."

"I've never lied, Eric. I've just never—"

"That's right. You're the one who doesn't put herself out there for others, aren't you? Not even for the father of your baby." He went to a secluded table in a far corner of the cafeteria and sat down. Then stood back up and pulled out a chair for her when Michi caught up to him. Damn old-world manners, he thought. Even for someone who'd done what she'd done.

"It was a bad pregnancy, Eric. I almost lost Riku several times. I was flat on my back for so long, not moving except when necessary, exam after exam, close calls… I spent most of the pregnancy after the first trimester in bed. And while that's no excuse for what I did, or didn't do, you do need to know what was going on with me. My intentions at the start were to let you know. But when it got bad…"

"I'm sorry for that," he said, his voice gentle. "I might not have been able to help, but I would have been there for you if I'd known. I'm not the kind of man who would turn my back on something like this."

"I was confused. Fighting a battle I didn't know how to fight. And after that one night together, remembering how adamant you were about not having any kind of involvement in your life, what was I supposed to do? Take you at your word, which was what I did? Or risk reaching out, only to be rejected? Emotionally, I wasn't up for that, Eric. I was fragile, and I wasn't able to handle any more than I already was."

"I'm sorry for what you went through, Michi. There are no words to express how I feel about that. But no matter what I'd told you, I had a right to know. Don't you understand that? Riku isn't just yours. He's mine, too. You carried my son for nine months, and now, two years later, the only reason I know anything is through a series of coincidences. What if we hadn't had that chance meeting in the coffee shop? Would you have gone back to Japan thinking you could save your secret for another time? Or forever?"

"The coffee shop might have been a coincidence, but I was going to tell you, Eric. I was struggling with how to do it. And, yes, not telling you would have been easier. Especially after making it through a bad pregnancy and hysterectomy, only to find out Riku was so ill. I think at that point I was beyond coping. It was all I could do to get myself from one moment to the next. But it was it was never my intention not to tell you. I just didn't know how or when. And I was scared…"

"Of what?"

"That you'd take him from me. Especially once you knew that he's…" She'd said it too many times, explained it too many times and now, when she most needed to say the words, she couldn't. Because this was the one time that mattered above all others. The time that could affect her and Riku for the rest of their lives.

"He's what, Michi? Tell me. What's going on?"

"Sick, Eric. Riku is really sick, and the real reason I'm here in New York is so he can have surgery. What you saw weren't cold symptoms. They were…" A lump formed in her throat as she struggled with the word. "They were the outward symptoms of his heart defect."

Eric blanched. "What?" he gasped.

Michi shook her head, then bit down hard on her bottom lip to keep herself from crying. "He has…" She drew in a deep breath. "He was diagnosed with truncus arteriosus with a ventricular septal defect. And, yes, I know that's your specialty. But since you couldn't be involved my aunt set it up with the doctor who will be performing the surgery. Dr. Anjali Kapoor."

"You asked her without consulting me first?"

"I've done a lot of things I should have done differently but, yes, I did. Now that you're not practicing, she's considered the best surgeon for Riku's condition, and I was lucky she agreed to do the surgery. With one less of you in the field, she's very busy."

"You let other people help, but not me? Why, Michi? I don't understand what made you think I'd take him away from you."

"I didn't think that…well, not seriously. But I'm so used to protecting him from everything now…"

"Including his father." He sighed. "Did it ever occur to you that my son might need me? That I might have an opinion on his surgery based on how that *was* my specialty when I practiced?"

"But you as good as told me you didn't want anybody in your life. That's all I could think of, Eric, as I went through the steps I had to take to make sure Riku was getting everything he needed. All I knew was that Riku had a mother who would give her life for him and a father who'd said he didn't want to be involved. There's a wide gap in there, and I simply didn't have the emotional stamina I needed to bridge it.

"I tried getting hold of you during my pregnancy and even after Riku was born, but I couldn't, and I didn't have the energy to keep trying. And before you ask why Agnes didn't try…she didn't know you were Riku's father. Not until much later. Not until his doctors had determined he would need surgery. By then… all I can say is I'm sorry. I could have tried harder, but everything I had in me went to Riku and there was nothing left over for anything else."

Eric opened his mouth to say more, but no words came out. He looked so angry and hurt. To find out he had a son, then shortly after to be told his son was ill—her heart did go out to him as the pain she saw on his face was what she'd put there. But it was done, her choices made, and she couldn't go back and change things, not even if she wanted to. "I wish we could have done this better," she said. "I'm sorry you found out about Riku this way."

Eric nodded, but still didn't speak.

"Oh, and in case you're wondering why I didn't have the surgery done earlier, Riku's cardiologist back home advised that since the surgery would entail two different procedures, we should wait until he was a little older, and a little larger. Otherwise I'd have had it done a long time ago. I know it's usually done early on, but I wasn't negligent about this, Eric. He's had good medical care since the day he was born."

Eric walked over to the cafeteria window and looked out on the parking lot. It was not yet morning, but the day shift workers were beginning to appear. Parking their cars, heading into the hospital. Reporting for duty. Business as normal, except for him. Because now nothing was normal. His life had just changed, and he didn't know what to do about it yet. There were no rules or guidelines for this sort of thing. And right now, he was feeling so... lost, like the way he'd always felt after one of his father's rejections. Lost, bewildered, scared. "How bad is he?" he asked on a discouraged sigh. "And don't hold back, Michi. Not this time."

She took a sip of her tea, now cold, and bit her lower lip. "He's a little behind in some of his development like speech, but overall he's been good. It's only been in the last few weeks that I've noticed any real physical changes in him. You know, the intermittent oxygen when needed, a little less energy than before, lack of appetite."

He turned his back to the window to face Michi. "I might not have done anything differently for Riku than you've done, but I could have supported you...assured you that you were doing the right things. So why, Michi? I know you had serious problems, but I still don't understand why you didn't try harder once he was born."

"Why?" She drew in a deep breath. "Why didn't I try harder? Because of you, Eric. You, better than most, know the kind of care that he's required. It's twenty-four seven. You move from one thing to the next without getting a break in between. But I've never minded any of that. Not one minute of it. But you…you didn't want the commitment. No strings attached. Sure, you might have jumped in at the start, but I wasn't convinced you had the long haul in you. Riku's care is the long haul now, and even after his initial surgery, all I could think of was what would happen when you decided it wasn't in you any longer to make the commitment to his care.

"Personally, I didn't need that kind of rejection but, more, Riku didn't need it. He needs people around him he can trust, and he's old enough to make those distinctions. But his daddy…" She shrugged. "The whole situation scared me. You scared me."

"Based on what?"

"Some of the things you said. But mostly your jump from being a surgeon to a property manager. At the seminar you were excited about expanding your practice. I could see it in the way you took in every last detail of physiatry. And I heard it in the questions you asked. Then, in the blink of an eye, you'd gone off in an entirely different direction. Sort of like the way you left me that night. There one minute, then sneaking off into the night the next.

"And you didn't even come to my last class, which told me you were already part of my past. Riku needed stability and I wasn't sure you could give that to him when what I heard from you was how you didn't want the commitment, then afterwards what I saw said the very same thing.

"With Riku, I needed a commitment. Maybe not a marriage or a relationship with me, but somebody who would stand beside me through all of it. But you were hopping from one thing to another, and in that I didn't see a man who would stay there for Riku, no matter what. What I saw, Eric, was a man who would go sneaking off into the night again."

"Did it ever occur to you to give me a chance?"

"It did. But I was…still am overwhelmed

and I couldn't add your commitment problem to my problems. And, yes, it hurt leaving you out, but there weren't a lot of options available to me—continue to pursue a man who'd already told me he didn't want a relationship of any kind or concentrate on giving Riku everything he needs. For the sake of my son—our son—I did the right thing. The only thing I could do. Or, at least, the only thing I *thought* I could do. And I'm sorry I hurt you. That was never my intention."

As various workers on the morning shift began to filter into the cafeteria for their coffee, Eric took hold of Michi's hand and led her down the hall to the nearest private room, which happened to be the hospital chapel. Dimly lit and very empty. After they'd seated themselves in the corner of the rear pew, he leaned his head back against the wall and closed his eyes.

"My dad and I always had a difficult relationship," he began. "My mother left when I was five. Walked out the door one day and never came back. I never knew why, and I was forbidden even to speak about it. Meaning, at age five, I knew what rejection felt like. So, raising me was up to the old man, and all he wanted was an heir, someone to take over where he eventually left off. Since I was his only child, that would have been me. Except that wasn't what I wanted. Being a surgeon was. That topic opened up more debates and arguments than I can remember over the years, and since my dad already wasn't a nurturer, and that's putting it mildly, it simply widened the gap between us.

"As a result, I was raised by a lot of people: teachers at the boarding school where he sent me so he wouldn't have to deal with me; any number of hired nannies; the school custodian when Dad forget to take me home for a holiday; the woman who came in twice a week to do laundry. I was up for grabs, basically. Anybody who wanted me for a minute or a day or a week could have me. That was my life when I was a kid. I had a father who didn't love me and, as a result, I was always afraid I'd turn out just like him. Kids do that, you know. Turn out like their parents."

"Which is why you were so adamantly against relationships?"

"I would never put another child through what I went through. No physical abuse. No deprivation of anything except the thing I wanted the most. So, my no-commitment policy, it protected me, but most of all it protected someone else from me. Someone I might have come to love dearly." He shifted his position, moved over toward Michi until he was just barely touching her. And she didn't pull away. Even that simple gesture gave him the encouragement he needed to tell her more.

"Anyway, prior to coming to your seminar it had probably been three months since I'd had any contact with my dad, which suited me just fine as he was putting more pressure on me to leave medicine and join the company. Since I'd lived with that most of my life, I was pretty well able to shut it out. But there was this little boy inside me who always tried to win his dad's favor, even though he knew it wouldn't happen. Then the little boy turned into a successful man who'd still never received the approval or even the acknowledgement he wanted. At the time of the seminar we were basically estranged. I'd had enough, and I think even he was getting tired of the back and forth.

"But that night—*our night*—I got a text telling me he'd died. No explanation, no nothing. Just the words, Your dad has died. Return home immediately to assume control of Hart Properties. From his lawyer, by the way. For all his money, and all his importance, he was alone in the end. But he still got what he wanted because I did go home and took over where he'd left off.

"At first, I kept telling myself it was temporary, that I'd find someone to replace me then go back to medicine. But the people I interviewed…they all seemed like a different version of my dad. And here was little Eric with an entirely different view of the way things should be. So, I stayed. Resigned my position at the hospital and took over the company, probably to show myself I wasn't my dad. Strange psychology, I know. But parents do shape who their kids turn out to be. Except I had this altruistic view, whereas he was simply about profit and loss."

"I'm sorry," Michi whispered, taking hold of Eric's hand.

"So am I. As much as we didn't get along, he didn't deserve to die alone, but he did. Then the thing I'd always told him I didn't want to happen happened. Everything he owned became mine, including the company...the company that had originally torn us apart. And the first thing I knew, people were counting on me. I controlled their jobs and, essentially in some way, their lives. Hundreds of people. At night, when I'd try to go to bed, I'd see their faces. They needed something from me. Something better than my dad had ever given. Long story short, I gave up me to become a different version of him. And as for the morning I left without saying goodbye... I didn't even realize I'd done that until I was halfway back to New York.

"I intended to call you, but the instant I stepped out of the corporate jet my new life started, and it overwhelmed me for months. There were several times, during that period, when I thought about calling, but I didn't because I thought, *What's the point?* I wasn't the man you'd met in Japan. In fact, much of the time I wasn't even the man I'd always known. And I wasn't happy about any of it, Michi.

"After that night together, like you, I'd thought we could have more. I wasn't sure what it would have been since I was still against ending up in a real relationship. But it was the first time in my life I'd ever allowed that thought in, and for a little while I was hopeful. Then after the text, let's just say that I gave up on anything I might have wanted in order to prove myself to a man who would never know. By the time I'd figured all that out, it was too late to do anything but follow my new course."

"A course that's not being true to who you are? Can that ever make you happy, Eric?"

"Well, you know what they say about not always getting what you want. Only in my case I think I was confused about what I wanted. In the end I realized that, after a lifetime of trying to get it, my dad's approval didn't matter. Not to him and certainly not to me. But by that time, I had too many people dependent on me for so many things that I couldn't simply walk away."

"Sounds like we both went directions we didn't anticipate."

"And I'm glad yours was the better direction," he said. "I'm still angry that you didn't include me, and that's something it's going to take me a while to work through, but you've been a good mother to Riku. And now I want to prove I can be just as good a dad."

Michi brushed back a tear falling down her cheek, and he brushed away the next one with his thumb. "He needs both of us together, you know." And she truly wanted that to come from both of them. But words and sentiments aside, she still wondered if she could count on him in the long term because if he did back away again, she could take the rejection. Riku couldn't, though. And he was her only consideration here. Not herself. Not Eric. Only Riku, and she would fight with everything inside her to protect him, even if that meant fighting Eric.

But he seemed to care. That was what she was counting on, and praying her judgment wasn't being skewed by one night when all her wishes had come true.

CHAPTER FIVE

HE'D HEARD ALL her words and now he was stuck trying to get himself through the maze of uncertainty so he could figure out what to do next. Not only did he have a son—something that thrilled him to bits—but his son was sick, something that scared him worse than he'd ever been scared in his life. Apart from getting Riku through his illness, could he be a good father to him? A real father? The kind of father he'd never had?

Certainly, he'd never had an example to follow, but loving that little boy could make up for everything he'd lacked in his life, if he got it right. That was the big question. Could he? Michi had been right when she'd reminded him of how he'd said he didn't want involvements. He hadn't, and he always put that out there first. He knew that and, to some extent, had even worked at perfecting it. *Here I am, my terms. Take it or leave it.*

Sure, it protected him. Kept him apart from anything more that could let him down. Yet that had changed the moment he'd found out about Riku. Instant love. Total, complete love for someone he hadn't even properly met.

So, yes, he did understand Michi's reasoning for keeping Riku a secret. To anybody on the outside, looking in, he was a sleight of hand trick. *Here I am but if you take too long to blink, I'll be gone.* But if you were on the inside, looking out…well, who was he kidding? He'd never yet let anybody get close enough to know him on the inside.

Still, to hide his son from him? Sick or not, that little boy was his, and he should have been included in both the good and bad of Riku's life. Not only because he already loved that kid, but because no child deserved to grow up so separated from either of his parents, the way he'd been separated. His dad's reasoning he understood up to a point. But his mother's… That was a wound that had never quite healed, and he didn't want Riku ever to have to deal with that.

OK, so maybe those considerations didn't belong here now, when Riku was on the verge of a major surgery, but there were so many different things to think about. Things that had never before entered his mind. His son's schooling. Would athletics be possible or would Riku be more the studious type? Or maybe an artist or musician? Would he go to university someday, and what would he study? Would he get married? Have a family of his own?

And Michi? What about Michi? He didn't want to hate her. Quite the opposite. But after what she'd done…

Well, one thing was sure. For now, he and Michi would unite for the sake of their son. Getting him through this surgery was the *only* thing that mattered. Everything else could be worked out later. "Is he susceptible to colds?" Eric asked, holding her hand, needing the feel of it in a way that was foreign to him. But

Riku was having another scan now and all he could do was wait. It was killing him.

"I don't take him out around too many people because I know his heart condition can suppress his immune system. So, I really can't answer that because he's been pretty sheltered so far."

"And did you choose anyone special to be on the surgical team, or did you leave that up to Dr. Kapoor?" This wasn't right. This conversation should be between two parents who were frightened for their child. Not one parent who was able to show her vulnerability and one who hid behind his medical knowledge. But it was safe there. Someplace he could count on. Someplace that had never let him down when everything else in his world had.

"Really, Eric. That's what you want to talk about? The surgical team?"

"My default, I guess."

"Riku doesn't need a default. He needs a dad. And, yes, you could argue that I've deprived him of that, and you'd be right. But that's not what it's about right now." She broke loose of his hold and walked over to the crib where Riku would be returned shortly. It was midmorning now, and the hospital was in its full daily swing.

"He has a crib at home that's decorated with baby animals. He's particularly fond of the giraffe. So I made a mobile to hang above his crib…all giraffes. Sometimes at night he'll wake me up giggling, and I'll know he's watching that mobile. It makes me feel…safe, hearing that giggle."

She turned around to look at him. "He has a beautiful giggle. When I hear it, I can almost forget what else goes along with it. But he's a normal little boy, Eric. Likes the things all toddlers his age do. And so often, when I look at him, I wonder if he wonders why he's not allowed to do those things. Or, at some point, will he resent me for not allowing him to do the things I know he'd love to do?"

He walked over to the crib but kept his distance as he didn't feel like he had the right to encroach. "Kids are resilient. I used to see that every day. One day they'd be so sick it would break your heart, then later, after surgery, they'd be up and about like nothing had ever been wrong in the first place. For me, that was always the best part. Seeing the way they bounced back."

He drew in a deep breath, resisting the urge to move a couple steps closer then pull her into his arms, but the mixed messages from that would only muddy a dire situation, and Michi didn't need to deal with any more than she already was. "He's not going to hate you. Well, except for when he turns into a teenager and those can be pretty trying years. But when he's mature enough, he will see the sacrifices you've made for him, and he'll come around."

"Not sacrifices," she said, wiping away tears streaming down her face. "Not when you love someone the way I do Riku. Then whatever you do to make their life better, or easier... that's what makes your life better as well."

Damn, she was a good woman. All the attributes he'd thought she had were there in abundance. And, yes, he had every right to be angry. But being angry at Michi...it just wasn't in him. It was all one big, conflicting mess. But watching her suffer, and knowing what she'd given up to take care of their son… it brought out feelings in him he'd never expected. Tender feelings. Caring feelings. Feelings of how he so desperately needed to help her he'd put himself through anything just to be close by.

"When is the surgery scheduled?" he asked, retreating to his safety zone because right now his feelings were too close to the surface and Michi didn't need to deal with them. He was used to doing it on his own. He would manage.

"Dr. Kapoor's lecturing in Dubai right now. If Riku can be put on a normal schedule, it'll be in four days. If it's decided he's an emergency…" She shrugged. "I suppose I should have had a back-up plan, but I didn't."

"Can I take care of that for you?"

"You can't operate, Eric. If you could, you would have been my first choice."

"But there's somebody…my mentor, actually. I'd like to give him a call and see if he'll come in if we need him."

"Do you trust him with your son's life, Eric?"

Eric nodded.

"Then do what you have to do because I trust you to make the right decision. I'm so tired of doing this alone. Mentally exhausted. And I need you, Eric. I need you to make decisions to get Riku through when I'm not capable of doing it any longer. Or even for a moment or two. Yes, any of my family would help. But Riku needs this from his father. And I need what Riku needs."

It wasn't Eric who stepped up to Michi but Michi who stepped up to Eric, and allowed herself to be pulled into his arms. And for the next several minutes they stayed that way. Like a family. Until a nurse poked her head in the door. "Just thought you should know, your little boy will be back in just a few minutes. The scan is over and as soon as the doctor finishes making his notes, he'll accompany Riku back here. Oh, and he's lightly sedated, so I think he'll be sleeping a while."

"I was hoping he'd be awake so you can

actually meet him and see just how wonderful he is," Michi said. Something that should have happened before now, but there was no going back, was there? No way to make amends for the pain she'd caused. So, at the moment, all she could do was move forward and keep hoping for a resolution that would benefit all three of them. "Look, Eric. I don't know how he's going to react to you, especially now that he's not feeling well. Like I said, I've sheltered him, so maybe you shouldn't expect too much this first time. Especially if he's groggy."

"Would you rather have me stay away?"

"No. Not at all. I just don't want you to be… disappointed. Or hurt. When he's not feeling well he can be moody."

"I know how to deal with sick children, Michi. I used to be very good at it."

"But this is different, Eric. He's your son and he might not respond to you the way you'd want. I just want you to be aware of that." Because she wanted this first real meeting between father and son to be perfect. It wouldn't make up for what Eric had been deprived of in the past, but it might give him some encouragement for the future if Riku responded well.

Suddenly it struck her that her investment in this situation wasn't just for Riku's sake. It was for Eric's as well. What he wanted, what he needed mattered so much she was surprised she hadn't seen that before now. Maybe it was another way to exclude him? Or maybe it was something more, something where she was afraid of where including Eric might take her.

"Does he know he has a father?"

Michi nodded. "I've mentioned it. Shown him where you worked. Told him what kind of man you are."

"If I speak to him in English, will he understand me?"

This time she shook her head. "We speak Japanese at home. That's what he understands."

"So basically I'll be a stranger who doesn't speak his language, which means there's no real reason for me to see him except that I want to."

"I think he'll know, Eric. Or at least he'll sense your feelings for him."

"I hope so," he said, holding out his hand to her and moving back toward the wall as the nurse wheeled the gurney through the door. She lifted Riku into the crib and began to attach wires, tubes and all manner of other medical equipment no child that age should ever have to know about. "He's doing well," she assured Michi and Eric, then exited the room as the doctor on the case entered.

"Well, the good news is, after comparing previous records to the results of the tests we've just taken, there's been no significant change," reported Dr. Leroy Watson, staff cardiologist. "I've sent everything to Dr. Kapoor and she agrees we should do what we can to keep him stable. Considering his condition, that's still a lot more than the little guy deserves, but I don't want to risk any setbacks." He looked at Eric. "Would you like to look at his test results?"

"I would, except I'm the dad in this one, not the doctor. So I probably shouldn't."

"Well, anyway... I expect he'll sleep the rest of the day. Probably most of the night, too. I'll leave the three of you alone. But if there's anything you need..."

"Thanks, Leroy," Eric said. "For what it's worth, I'm glad you're going to be his hospitalist."

Leroy chuckled. "You should be, since you're the one who requested me."

Michi looked up at Eric. "Seriously?"

"OK, I can't be my son's doctor, and we all know why. But I sure as hell can get the best doctors to look after him."

"And I blush," Leroy said, taking a bow then backing out of the room.

"Without telling me, Eric?"

"Let me contribute something, Michi. You just told me to help you make decisions, and that's what I did. I talked to Leroy, who had an opening, and I jumped on it because he's in high demand. He's good. No, he's damned good and I didn't want to miss the chance to have him take over Riku's normal care. I mean, there's not much else I can do right now except find the best for Riku. So, if you're angry..."

She stepped up to him, stood on tiptoe, and kissed his cheek. "Not angry. Grateful. But obviously still on autopilot for overreacting."

"Overreacting accepted. Overprotective accepted as well. You're the kind of parent Leroy and I love working with."

"Not possible," she said, smiling. "Back in Japan, I made the lives of several of his doctors miserable with my ways. I didn't mean to, but sometimes I couldn't help myself."

He chuckled. "OK, so maybe I'll take back the 'love working with' part and change it to *appreciate* working with. Or *respect* working with. Or *fear* working with. Or run away from totally."

Michi smiled. "All right. I get your point and I'll try hard to do better here. But be warned..."

"Duly noted," he said. "And I'll have Leroy mark in Riku's chart that his mother has an overabundance of overbearing and overprotective tendencies. Will that work for you?"

"I think I'm beginning to understand why you were considered so good. Sure, you had your OR skills, but you top them with your nonsense skills."

"I aim to please, ma'am. I surely do aim to please. And now, on a serious note, will you tell me about him? I want to know everything. His likes, dislikes. Favorite food. What kinds of toys does he play with? His personality. Everything..." Spoken like a man with a desperate need to know.

"Anything you want," she said, reaching into the crib to take hold of Riku's hand.

"We certainly did make a beautiful boy," Eric said, standing back just enough to catch the entire picture of mother and son. "And there are so many things I want to do with him when he's better."

"You said when," she said, choking back the tears that so badly wanted to fall. "You said *when*, not *if*. Everybody has said... Even Dr. Kapoor said if. But you said..." She swallowed hard as the tears fell despite her best effort to hold them back. "I know people don't mean anything by it, but it hurts, Eric. Nobody knows how badly."

"I think I can guess," he said, resisting the urge to pull her into his arms. It might have been the decent thing to do, but he wasn't sure what Michi wanted, or expected of him. And now didn't seem the time to overstep, even though that's what he wanted to do. Pull her into his arms, hold her, reassure her. All mixed feelings, to be sure. Feelings he wasn't yet ready to explore. Not until he had sorted some of his own confusion.

"Michi, I've never seen any of my patients in terms of *if*. It's always *when* because that single, simple word gives hope, and not just to the parents and family but to me as well. And because this is my son, I refuse to believe anything but *when*. I want to figure out what kind of future I'll have with him *when* he's better. I know he'll have some restrictions, and there'll be another surgery or two in the future, but he's going to have that future. That's what I'm going to think no matter what anybody else says. It's what I have to think. What we both have to think."

"I want to make us work. Maybe not as a family but as two adults who love one child… love him more than anything else in life. And I do want to think in terms of *when*. I try hard to, but then I get scared, or someone says something, or, like now, Riku gets sick, and nothing makes sense. I panic when he sneezes, Eric. Or when he isn't as responsive as I think he should be.

"I watch every little thing he does and read more into what I'm seeing than I should. I can't sleep in my own bed because I have to be in the chair next to his bed. And I can't turn off the lights at night in case he does something, or something happens to him I can't see. That's the life I've been living ever since he was born. I miss more work than I should. I never go out with friends. I don't even make it to dinner most of the times my family gets together because I don't like Riku being around so many people. And masks…"

Eric chuckled. "Seriously? You ask people to wear masks around him?"

"Not my family so much anymore. But when he was first diagnosed I did. I carried spares in my pockets, just in case."

"And it was your choice to do it all alone?"

"It was the only thing I knew to do. For me, these past few years have been a struggle just getting from day to day. I've devoted everything I am to get *him* through. Not me. Him. Which, of course, I made a mess of, didn't I?" She pushed herself back from the crib a little, then looked up at him. Saw a look on his face that broke her heart. "I never meant to hurt you," she said, reaching up to brush his cheek with her hand.

"But you did," he said, his voice sounding so broken it barely escaped him. "And I haven't figured out what to do about that yet, Michi, because there's already been too much pain."

Her stomach churned. She couldn't blame him for what he was feeling, and in so many ways she loved him for trying to hold it back. Most people wouldn't have done that. But, then, Eric wasn't most people. "Eric, since Riku's going to sleep for a while, could we get out of the hospital? I've spent so much time in them, not just working but with Riku, I'd simply like to get out for a few minutes and take a walk. Maybe Agnes will come sit with him while we're gone."

"Do you want me to go ask her?"

Michi shook her head. "No, you stay here with your son. I'll go talk to her and meet you back here in a few minutes."

The night was cool but not cold. Jacket weather, not coat. Michi loved the crispness of it, and the sense that the slight chill brought about new hope. "Thank you," she said to Eric. "It's been so long since I've simply stepped away from everything, I can't even remember when the last time was." She drew in a deep breath of air and let it out slowly. "Maybe three years or more." She laughed. "In fact, I think you were my last step away."

"Then I should be flattered."

"Are you?" she asked.

"More than you could know."

Standing with Eric at the top of the hospital steps, Michi looked at the street down below, to the congestion of traffic and the masses of people walking almost shoulder to shoulder, trying to get to wherever they were going. No one seemed perturbed. In fact, everyone in her view seemed to take whatever came their way in stride. It would be wonderful to live life that way, she thought. Standing in the middle of so many people going so many different ways, and no one seeming to care about the distractions and misdirecting.

"Do you ever have the urge to simply be part of the crowd? Get yourself lost in it for a while and let it sweep you along to wherever it's going?"

"Occasionally. More so now than when I was younger. My structure now is…different."

"But wouldn't it be nice to be on your own for a bit? No cares, no worries. No responsibilities. Especially no responsibilities, except to yourself."

"You do have to take care of yourself sometimes. Give in to the pressure and simply… breathe. And I understand that when you have a child, your child always comes first. But there's room in your life for you as well, Michi. Now that I'm here, I'll make sure you find it whenever you need to."

"I wouldn't really want to be on my own. Not without Riku. But you're right. Sometimes I don't really feel like there's much room for me now in my own life." She looked up at the sky, and through the maze of New York city lights she could see the black sky and a smattering of twinkling stars. "That's what people keep telling me, but…"

Eric chuckled. "But you're stubborn." He took her by the arm and led her down the hospital walkway to the sidewalk. "You always do it your way."

Slow steps, deliberate. Allowing her time to take in the things that had eluded her for so long. She was so keenly aware of his presence she tingled from his touch even through her jacket. "Or not stubborn as much as dedicated, as I would prefer to call it." Across the street, a vendor cart seemed to float in a halo of steam as people lined up to buy whatever was being sold.

"Usually hot coffee, tea, hot cider or hot cocoa," Eric said, as if reading her mind. "Which would you prefer?"

Coffee and tea were everyday. Cider wasn't to her liking. But sipping hot cocoa on a chilly night while walking along the teeming street on the arm of the most handsome man in the crowd...how could she resist that? Moments of fancy or even fanciful romance didn't come along for her too often and she was in the mood for a bit of that now. But only for this one moment in time. That's all she could allow. "Cocoa, please," she said.

"Then let's make that two hot cocoas," he said to the vendor, then looked at Michi. "With or without marshmallows?" he asked.

"Marshmallows. In Japan we have what's called the blooming marshmallow that unfolds as a flower on top of the hot chocolate." She laughed. "Funny. I haven't thought of that in years."

"Then we'll have to make sure Riku has his first blooming marshmallow experience when he's well enough to drink it." Eric handed Michi her paper cup of hot cocoa and pointed to the carriage sitting empty just down the street. "Care for a ride?" he asked.

The horse was white, its tail braided with shiny blue streamers. The carriage was white as well, decorated in the same shades of blue as the horse's tail. "As many times as I've been to New York, I've never done that." And doing it for the first time with Eric seemed perfect. The way everything seemed perfect right now.

"Then I think it's time for your first ride."

"You don't think it's too chilly?"

"You've got your hot cocoa to keep you warm, as well as the blanket the driver will offer us once we get in. And if neither of those work, you've always got me."

Suddenly the image of a snuggle with Eric was all she could think about. And before she could blink, they were in the back of the horse-drawn carriage, its top up, and clopping their way slowly down the road toward Central Park as the coachman in front chattered on merrily about the various buildings and sights they were passing.

To Michi, it felt like she and Eric were stepping back in time to a place where the honking horns didn't exist, and the people on the street were all lovers, walking arm in arm. OK, so maybe she was waxing too romantic, but that was an image that seemed to belong there. To her. To them, as they sat shoulder to shoulder, meandering through Central Park while the soft jostle of the carriage rocking to the gait of the horse, the placid, mesmerizing sound of hooves on pavement turned into just the balm she needed to soothe her soul. And for Michi, in that time, the coachman didn't exist. It was just Eric and her. Her eyes, her senses, her awareness only of him.

"Are you enjoying this?" he asked.

"You don't know how much. If I could make time stop right here for just a little while..." She smiled at him. "Be careful what you wish for, right?"

"You're allowed a wish for yourself," he

said, as the coachman slowed for one of the park entrances.

"Care to get out?" the coachmen asked, turning very slowly in his seat, as if to be unobtrusive. Perhaps that was the instruction given to coachman when they believed they carried lovers. Blend in, make the ride about them, not you. Don't interrupt what appears to be a private moment.

Eric looked over Michi. "We could ride a while longer or take a walk. Your choice."

"I'd love to walk," she said. Hand in hand. Maybe lingering by one of the reflecting ponds, echoing exact images from their edges. Or strolling through one of the many dimly lit tunnels where untold kisses had been stolen or offered up freely. "I've never done that here, after dark. It always seemed so sad, being alone here, maybe the only person without a lover or someone to walk with them."

"Wishes again?" he asked, as he helped her out of the carriage.

"More like observations, I think. And maybe guesses." She'd never had anyone in her life she'd considered a lover. Acquaintances, dates, friends, but no lovers until Eric. And she wasn't considering lover in the sexual sense as much as an intimate sense. In her life, Eric was the only man she'd ever felt close to.

After handing the coachman a generous tip, he took hold of Michi's hand and pulled her over to the trail, then led her to the top of the steps leading down to the reflecting pond, where the twinkling stars above seemed to join with the water as sparkling shards. Champagne glasses. Pure crystal. Diamonds. Eric simply stood there a moment, looking down at her. "Someone like you should never be alone here, Michi," he finally said.

"And that would be your wish?" she asked him.

"No, this would be." He stood, legs braced to receive her weight, and the chill of the night air, as if by magic, wove a spell around them, binding them together to seek the warmth they each had to offer. Her arm, pressed to his, burnt like a slow, smoldering ember, piercing the layers of his jacket and shirt and on through the rest of him, like he was mere air, powerless to stop the burning of it. Not that he would, even if he could. "You know, we always do our best kissing at night," he said, his voice raspy with desire.

"We've done our only *real* kissing at night," she replied.

"A nice habit to repeat." Eric shifted slightly and for a moment Michi wavered, off balance. But he caught her quickly, pulling her into his arms then bending his face to meet hers. Her dark eyes were caught in a moment of indecision. Should she? Shouldn't she? But the questions were hers to answer, not his. "If that's the kind of habit you like," he said, his lips only a heartbeat away from hers.

"Habits can be good," she said. "So can spontaneity."

"Either or," he said as his lips met hers, and his grip on her tightened, pulling her into him even more while she pressed herself to him with the same eagerness.

The tip of his tongue brushed hers and she opened to let him in as he welcomed the urgency that sent a wildfire racing through every nerve, every sinew of his body. It was Eric who was left weak in the knees, overcome by sheer want for her. It was also Eric who held onto her for dear life. That at first frightened Michi, as she tensed up and backed ever so slightly away from him.

"It's all right," he said. "Just relax and listen to your heart." He chuckled. "Even if it's telling you something entirely different from what your head is saying. Which it probably is if what I'm feeling is anything close to what you're feeling."

"But I don't know how to make my head stop," she said, glancing over at the group of people walking around them, giving them a wide berth. Laughing quietly as if they knew something she didn't. "As much as I'd like it to sometimes. But it's like I can't shut down. I'm always on alert. My mind going in so many directions. Sometimes I wish time would slow down or simply stop long enough to let me catch my breath before I have to move on to the next challenge."

"As much as we'd like it to, time doesn't stand still. Unfortunately, you must play its game as it will never play yours. And its game is sometimes cruel. I'm sorry that's the case for you, that you're not able to enjoy all the moments given you, especially with Riku. But soon, after the surgery…."

"I hope so," she said, trying to hide the look in her eyes, which she knew would betray her need. But she'd fought the battle to hold everything back from everyone for so long that just this once she wanted to let go. Let her vulnerability take over. Lean on someone else… Eric. "Because doing this alone…"

In the catch of a breath he took her lips, his late-in-the-day beard rough against her skin. A faint moan escaped Michi's lips and he could feel her resistance begin to melt away, causing the level of his heat to rise, to burn in his chest, his face, his lips, everywhere. It was like his will had surrendered to hers, getting itself tangled in her hesitancy. Wanting more yet fearing more would send her skittering away. "I, um…" he said, backing away. "Care to go ice skating?"

Michi blinked hard, looking up at him in disbelief. "Ice skating?" she asked.

He confirmed her question with a nod.

"Why?" she asked.

"It's safe. And right now I really need safe."

He needed to be safe while she was willing to take the risk. Well, she deserved that, didn't she? Probably should have seen it coming. Michi laughed, not because it was funny but because of the sheer frustration building up inside her. "Habitually or spontaneously?"

"Maybe a little bit of both, where you're concerned."

"So, do they rent skates here?" she asked, holding her hand out to take his. As athletic as he was, or used to be, Eric's skating was over in less than five minutes. No tumbles to the ice, but he was getting pathetically close to it, and he wanted to look better than that. For Michi. He didn't give a damn about the other hundred skaters on the ice, all in their various stages of taking their own tumbles. All except for Michi. She was graceful. Like a swan. Floating over the ice, casting a spell that made her appear to glide above it. And the smile on her face... In this moment, she had no cares, no worries. She was simply there, wrapping herself in the bliss of pure abandon, no thought of the world that would come crashing back soon enough.

Despite their problems, if he hadn't fallen a little in love with her before, he surely would have now, watching the pure magic she spun over everything. Including him. After nearly ten minutes of indulging himself in watching her, he took to the ice again, catching up to her not as quickly as he would have liked. She stopped when he finally did and smiled. "I'm out of shape," she said, barely winded.

"If that's what you consider out of shape, I'd love to see what you consider *in* shape."

"You did," she said, holding out her hand to him. "Here, let's do this together."

"I'll hold you back," he warned, knowing

that nothing in Michi's life should ever hold her back from anything she wanted.

"Maybe I'll hold you back."

He shook his head. But didn't say a word. Instead, he took hold of her hand, and in mere moments they were sailing over the ice together, smoothly, effortlessly. The way he wanted their lives to be. Until…

Michi looked down at him, sprawled flat, staring up at the sky. Then laughed. "One of life's little bumps," she said, as he refused her offer to help him back up. So instead she took out her phone and snapped a photo.

"Seriously?" he asked, once he was up, brushing ice crystals off his back side.

"For Riku. To put in the scrapbook of his life." She winked. "Or maybe in the scrapbook of mine. You're not there yet, you know."

"And this is where you want me to start?"

"This is absolutely where I want you to start. Foibles, falls and all."

CHAPTER SIX

AN HOUR AFTER the ice rink had closed, they were back to life as normal, and Michi felt herself go weak in the knees with the latest news. But before she tumbled to the floor, Eric put a steadying arm around her like it was simply something he always did. "You OK?" he whispered to her.

She nodded. "It's not easy." But Eric did make it easier and for that she was grateful.

"As you know, it's all part of the defect he has," Leroy continued, holding out a bottle of water for Michi without missing a beat. "But oxygen's easy enough to supplement and I've ordered blood gases drawn, so until we know more…" He looked at Eric. "Wish I could do better. But I think his surgery needs to be moved up. That's your decision, of course.

Oh, and I've made Dr. Kapoor aware of the downturn in his condition."

"Minor downturn," Michi challenged. In Riku's life there were upturns and downturns. A problem with his oxygen levels was only one of so many things she had to monitor. She looked at Eric. "So, about your back-up plan…"

"And this is where I leave the two of you to your discussions." With that, Dr. Leroy Watson prepared for one of his well-known grand gesture departures by kissing Michi's hand. "Call me if you have questions. We'll make sure there's an OR available when you decide what to do."

Amidst the strife, Michi did smile. "Were you ever that bold when you were practicing?" she asked. "Because I like his form."

"For me, bold was stepping out from behind my mask. Despite his demeanor, Leroy is as good as they get. A good old country GP trapped in a big-city hospital."

"Well, for what it's worth, the little personal touch makes a difference."

She stood there for a moment, looking at Riku, who was now under an oxygen tent. He was sleeping peacefully, no stress or pain showing on his face. "He's a fighter, Eric," she said, biting her lower lip. "But how long can a person fight before it just wears them down too much?"

He slid his arm around her shoulder and pulled her into him. "It's time, Michi."

She swallowed hard and nodded. "I suppose I knew that when Agnes called us to come back. Riku's ready, and so am I." She looked up at him. "What about you? Because this is about you, too."

"I want my son healthy. Dr. Kapoor would have been a good choice, but I can have Henry Johnston here inside three hours."

"And he's your back-up plan?"

"My mentor. A man I'd trust with the life of my son."

"Then get him here. I know he'll want to run tests first, so the sooner the better. OK?"

This time Eric was the one to swallow hard

and nod. "I'll have the corporate jet off the ground as soon as Henry's ready to fly."

"It's the right thing, isn't it?"

"For all of us, Michi."

Michi was taking it all in, and she understood everything that went on in the next little while. Eric's friend was getting himself ready to come to New York. More tests were being ordered. Agnes was co-ordinating with the surgery department. Her parents were on their way over from Japan. There was a flurry of activity suddenly. But watching her baby sleep, it was like she was floating over and above all this and looking down on Riku, seeing him as a perfectly normal, healthy child. She was pushing him on a baby swing. Helping him build sand castles. Sailing balsa boats with him on the pond. Feeding ducks. Going barefoot in the grass.

"Did you hear me, Michi?" Agnes asked.

She heard her name and blinked herself back to reality only to find Eric holding her hand now. "What?" she asked.

"Dr. Watson has written the order to move

him to the pediatric intensive care unit until we get the surgical arrangements made. As a precaution, though. Only as a precaution."

"Then I'm glad he's going to have twenty-four-hour care for a while." She looked at Eric, who was simply standing off by himself, staring out the window now. "It's a good thing, isn't it, Eric?"

He sucked in a shuddering breath. "It's another cog in the wheel. First the PICU, then the surgery, then the road to recovery. So, yes, it's a good thing."

She studied him for a moment, her heart aching for the pain he was experiencing. And it was she who went to his side, took his hand, and simply stood with him as the transport technicians and nurses prepared Riku for his next big move.

"I've always known this moment would come. Of course, I've wanted to delay it. I know about the procedure, what it involves. Watched videos, studied every movement a good surgeon should make. Considered every way it could go wrong, and every way it could go right. All preparing me for what will be happening shortly. I can quote you statistics, I can quote you long-term goals for children with Riku's heart defect. Successes. Failures. If it's out there, I've read it, hoping that when the time came I would be ready. But I'm not." She sniffed back a tear.

"Knowing what I know doesn't make things easier, and I can't even begin to imagine what you're going through, being the best in the world at this procedure yet standing aside feeling virtually helpless. And that's what you're feeling, Eric, because that's what I'm feeling. All the medical knowledge in the world and none of it will help our little boy."

"The first time I performed the procedure, it was the best feeling in the world, giving normalcy to a young life that had seen very little of it. Everybody told me the first one was the best and after that it all becomes routine. But it never was. For me, there was always a thrill seeing blood coursing through a tiny body the way it should. Seeing a sick child become vibrant in almost the blink of an eye. Knowing that in a very short time that child would be living a normal life, doing normal things. Experiencing life in a way he or she never had before. And to be part of that..."

"Didn't it kill you, walking away from it all?"

"It did. I used to love getting up in the morning knowing my little bit of effort that day could change a life. Then, when all that stopped, I still got up in the morning, but there was nothing to love. At least, not the way I loved being a surgeon." He chuckled bitterly.

"So, here I am on the other end of it now, and the only thing I can think is I wish to God I could be the one to do this. It's like my not doing this is letting him down. Funny, the things we think about in a crisis. I know Henry is the best possible surgeon we can get. I know this hospital has the very best in all the latest technology to make this a huge success and help Riku along in his progress. But I still feel like such a damn failure."

They stepped aside as Riku's bed, along with his unplugged monitoring equipment, was rolled to the door. "You're not a failure, Eric. How can you be, when you were never even given the chance to know your son? Or to succeed at anything with him? And I'm so, so sorry for that."

"Well, regrets don't really get us anywhere, do they?" he said, taking hold of her hand and walking out the door with her, then to the elevator and to the pediatric intensive care unit, where Riku was being settled in.

He was still sleeping, thankfully breathing easily. For that, Michi was grateful. It was a good sign. And she was grateful to lean on Eric for support. That was also a good sign. And soon, maybe very soon, they could face happy prospects and talk about being a family. That was what she had to keep in mind. They were a family now, in some fashion or form, and Riku made that possible.

The rooftop garden was lush, and much larger than he remembered it being when he'd worked here. It was mostly planted with autumn vegetables now—squash, a few late tomatoes, kale, carrots, beets, second-harvest lettuce. All the right ingredients for a salad. But it was a teaching area, a place to train children about nutrition and re-acquaint adults with wholesome foods they might have forgotten. Eric used to take his breaks here, come outside to get away from the hospital atmosphere and the incessant worry of the operating room, and simply think. Or, in some cases, try not to think. Today it was a little bit of both.

"Someone's put a lot of effort into expanding it," he said to Michi, who was sitting on the garden wall, sipping hot tea. They'd spent the night in Riku's room, neither of them sleeping, and now, in what most would consider the still wee hours, the final prep for surgery was underway. Henry was here, ordering the tests he wanted, even though many were repeats of what had already been done. But he was thorough and, with Riku's life in his hands, Eric was glad for that.

"That would be my aunt, although she doesn't want anybody to know it. She started this garden as a retreat just for frazzled doctors, and over the course it turned into something significant. I've done the same at my parents' hospital, and it's amazing the way children respond when they're given the opportunity to learn then invest that knowledge in something they can see growing. Riku loves the garden. When the weather's good, I take him there as often as I can."

"Does he eat the vegetables?"

"Sometimes. But only if he picks them. That's the part he loves best, I think. Finding a little cherry tomato, plucking it from the vine then eating it as his reward. He likes sweet red peppers, too. I think it's all about the color, because if he doesn't go for something red, orange is his next favorite. Except carrots. He hates carrots. But he loves sweet potatoes. So, if he finds one, he gets so excited when we take it home and I cook it up for him. Sweeten it a little, then sprinkle on a bit of cinnamon and he's in heaven. But you should have seen him the time he dug up a radish. Not sure who planted them, or why, but he loved it because it was red, and he fussed until I let him take a bite. Then it was like his whole world turned upside down in one little bite."

"What happened?" Eric asked.

Michi pulled her phone from her pocket and searched for a video. The one where Riku was having a bit of a temper tantrum, angry at the radish, looking at it like he couldn't believe it had betrayed him. Then finally trying to re-bury it in the dirt. "He has a temper some-times," she said, laughing at a video she had laughed at a hundred times before.

"Can't blame him, expecting something to be one way only to find out you're entirely wrong. I'd have buried it back in the dirt, too."

"He's going to love having you as a father," she said.

"And that doesn't scare you?"

"Of course it does. Turning control of my son over to anyone scares me. But for the first time I see Riku's future and I finally under-stand there must be more than me in it. A sick baby needs his mom, but a rambunctious tod-dler, which is what he's going to be, needs more than that."

"Michi, I'm not the sort who'll get tangled up in the parent thing for a while then back off it. I know that's what you're afraid of because all you've seen of me is how I back off. From surgery. From one night we both know should have been more. I keep thinking if I'd only woken you up and told you why I had to go we might not be where we are now. And I'm not talking about Riku. I mean, maybe you would have trusted me more when you found out you were pregnant, even come to me for support.

"But what you saw was a man who was always backing out the door. And while that's not my nature, it's all you had to go by. So, I do understand your doubts about me.

"But, please, don't assume that I'll back out the door once I've had enough of being a father. I'll admit it scares me. I don't have a very good example to follow. But if love counts for anything, I do love that little boy with all my heart."

"It was never about you being his father, Eric. It was about you deciding you didn't want to be his father. I didn't want my son starting off his life being rejected, and I wasn't sure you wouldn't do that."

"What do you think now?"

"I think you mean what you say."

"But?"

"But I need to take this one step at a time. I'm not going to keep you away from your son, but I don't know how we're going to work out the details yet. And right now I can't think about that."

"Fair enough," he said. "But just so you know, I'm in this all the way, Michi. Not just for Riku but for you."

"That's what I want. I really do. But, like I said, now's not the time for this to be happening. I can't deal with more than I already am. And in the meantime, I have a toddler to get ready for the day, even though the day is about more pre-surgery tests. We have this little ritual every morning, if you'd care to be part of it."

"Are you sure you want me there? Or if Riku would want me there? Because as much as I want to be part of everything, I also don't want to disrupt his life, especially in the things he's come to count on."

"Maybe it's time to let him see how he can count on you."

"So, what's this morning routine?" he asked.

"After the normal bath, breakfast things, we do 'The Wheels on the Bus.' Do you know that song?"

"In English?"

She shook her head, laughing. "Not unless you teach him the English version. But now it's all about the Japanese."

"And I'll look silly, not knowing it."

"Maybe if you just do the hand gestures while I sing."

"Only if I can teach him 'Mary Had a Little Lamb.'"

"He already knows that. In Japanese."

"'Twinkle Twinkle, Little Star'?"

"In Japanese."

"How about 'The Poor Father Who Couldn't Speak Japanese'? Does he know that song?"

"Not yet. But give him time. He'll figure it out."

"That's what I was afraid of."

"So, are you in or out?"

"Where Riku's concerned, you don't have to ask. And the title of that song in English is 'I'll Be There.'"

"I hope so, Eric. I really hope so."

"Would you like a glass of water or maybe a cup of tea?"

Michi was sitting in the rocking chair next to the crib, holding Riku and singing a quiet song to him while Eric put away the baby lotion and bathing supplies. He almost hated to disturb that moment, it was so beautiful, but Michi wasn't taking care of herself. And as this was, essentially, his first time with his son, he was nervous, and he hoped Riku wouldn't sense that.

"I would love some tea, but I think I'd like to go get it for myself while you sit here with him."

It was still early morning, but activities were picking up. Doctors on rounds. Nurses starting their assigned duties. Dietary bringing food, not so much for the tiny patients but for the parents who sat vigil and didn't take care of themselves. Parents like Michi, who looked so tired and pale as the morning light peeked through the blinds and betrayed her exhaustion. She'd borne this burden for so long alone, it was showing on her. Yet she wouldn't stop, not for a minute. Wouldn't even slow down. "Are you OK to do that? You look…"

"Tired?" she asked. "I've been tired for a while now. And there's only one cure." She scooted to the edge of the chair and gestured Eric over to her. "He's not a very sound sleeper, so don't worry if you wake him. He sleeps when his body tells him it's time."

"And your body?" he asked, lifting Riku gently into his arms, then stepping aside as Michi stood up.

"As the commercial on television says, it keeps on ticking. I'm fine, Eric. I appreciate your concern, but I've learned how to get through almost anything." She headed to the door. "Can I bring you anything?"

"I don't need anything, but you do, so why don't you go find a place to sleep for a while?"

"I… I don't sleep well if I'm not near Riku. And I really do want to be here when Henry comes back with the test results."

"Well, go do what you need to do, but don't worry. I'm here. Riku will be fine."

"I know that," she said, smiling. "Just be patient with me for a little while. It's difficult adjusting to having one more person involved, and that's my problem to overcome. Not yours."

Riku opened his eyes and looked up at Eric, stared at him for a moment, then snuggled in against his chest. "We'll work it out, Michi. But you do need to take care of yourself. So, go find a quiet place to sleep, and I'll call you when we know something. Doctor's orders," he said, smiling.

"Thank you, Doctor. You're too good. You know that, don't you?"

"I hope I come someplace close to that," he said. "Maybe in time I will. Oh, and thank you for the father-son time."

She took one long look, smiled, then turned and walked away. She was a good mother to

Riku. The best. No mother could have given more and he was grateful for that. And maybe somewhere inside that gratitude he would find the forgiveness she needed. Because the more he saw of her, and the more he saw her devotion, the more he was beginning to understand what a rough situation she'd been in almost from the moment they'd slept together.

The fight in her spirit…that was certainly new to him. So was the fierceness with which she took care of their son. While there'd been a time when he'd thought he could fall in love, what he was feeling now was admiration and even pride. Michi was everything he'd thought he'd loved, and so much more.

"You have a pretty great mother," he said to Riku, who was staring up at him. "But in your own way I'm sure you already know that. What I'm hoping is that, in time, you'll also come to realize you have a pretty great dad, because that's what I intend to be to you. Everything that my father wasn't to me. I promise you that, Riku. However this works out,

I'll be a part of your life." A substantial part, he hoped.

"So, what do we do now? Do you go back to sleep while your daddy sits here and rocks you? Or do we have a man-to-man talk? Your choice, little man. Because anything you want to do, your daddy wants to be part of it."

Riku's response was to squirm in Eric's arms, then mumble a couple of words Eric didn't understand. "What's that? You want your daddy to teach you how to play baseball? When you're older and you understand how to moderate yourself in your activities, I can certainly do that. And teach you to swim. Maybe we'll go camping. Do you think you'll love nature? It sure is a beautiful world out there now that you're in it."

Tears welled up in Eric's eyes as Riku smiled at him. Such a beautiful smile. Such a beautiful boy. An old song came to mind, one he remembered his mother singing. Something about baby resting his head close to mommy or daddy's heart, never to part... And, as he sang the song quietly, the words rang so true because he wouldn't part, not from Riku.

Outside, in the hall, standing just to the side of the door so he wouldn't see her, tears streamed down Michi's face. The song Eric was trying to recall was the song Riku loved the most. "Baby Mine." Eric was going to be a wonderful father to Riku. She sniffled back more tears then headed off to find a place to sleep. For the first time in ever so long she knew she would. Riku was safe with Eric and Eric would give his life for his son. Of that, she had no doubt.

"I put him back in his crib about an hour ago," Eric said. He was leaning on the hall wall outside Riku's room so as not to waken him. "We talked for about an hour, then he finally went back to sleep. And you?"

"Two blissful hours. Thank you."

"We're in this together, you know. When you need to sleep, or simply get away for a little while, I'll stay with him if that's what you want." She looked rested, but not enough, and if he could, he would have taken her back to his house, put her to bed, maybe gone to bed with her simply to hold her, and let her sleep as long as she needed. But Michi wasn't going to do that, and he understood the reason. Even two hours with his son made him realize there were so many responsibilities ahead—ones he didn't know about, ones his father had never taken seriously with him. And being there when your child was sick was one of the most important.

"I appreciate that, but you've got to understand it's hard letting go. Earlier…that was the first time I've ever walked away from him and left him in the hands of someone other than my family."

"But I'm Riku's family."

"I know. And I think Riku knows as well. But it's still difficult for me. So, any test results yet?"

"I just talked to Henry, as a matter of fact, and he'll be here shortly to discuss options with us."

"What kind of options?" she asked, her voice

now on the edge of panic. "I thought at this point we just do the surgery."

"Well, Henry has his ways. He's very methodical." He looked into Riku's room and his gaze went immediately to the monitors. Old habits. "He's on an up and down curve right now. That's why he's on the infant cannula for oxygen now instead of being in the tent. He's showing improvement, Michi, which is a good thing, especially with surgery coming up so soon."

"I was hoping you'd tell me my miracle baby had experienced some kind of miracle cure."

"That's what the surgery is. And once you finally get to meet Henry, I think you'll be a lot more confident."

"If he's anything like Leroy Watson, I'm sure that will make me feel better."

"So, you like your men bold?"

"I knew a bold man once."

"And?"

"And he became a terrific father. Story still in progress."

"You mean the part where you stood out in

the hall for fifteen minutes, listening to my pathetic attempt at a lullaby."

"Very bold," she said.

"Very bad," he responded. "And I think the only reason he went to sleep so easily was so he wouldn't have to listen to me."

"Or because he felt safe. 'Baby of mine.' That's his favorite, Eric."

"My mother used to sing it," he said. "It's one of the few things I remember about her, to be honest. I think the song made me feel…"

"Safe, the way it makes Riku feel. You have a good fathering instinct. I know you don't trust that yet, but it's there."

"How about we go back into the room, take our respective recliners and wait for Henry?"

As the sun peeked in through the blinds, it was Eric who dozed off while Michi stayed awake, marveling at how right this felt. Her two men sleeping while she kept watch over them. Except for the circumstances, it would have almost been perfect.

CHAPTER SEVEN

"I can't believe it's so late," Eric said, stretching his back.

"It's ten," she said.

"I'm assuming in the morning." This was the part about being a surgeon he didn't miss. The off-on schedule. Sleep for an hour or two. Operate. Do rounds. Doze. Back at it. It almost felt like he'd never left his practice because there'd been days where he literally hadn't known if he'd been waking up at night or during the day. Loss of orientation was one of the hazards of the profession. Back then. Not now. His day, his company, his people carried on whether he was there or sleeping in at home. Which he didn't do...force of habit. But the difference was that in one place he'd been essential, in another place he wasn't so much.

"In the morning, and Henry stopped in a little while ago. He didn't want to disturb your sleep, so he'll be back as soon as I text him." She handed him a cup of coffee and pointed to a plate with pastries. "Courtesy of my uncle. He sent them over earlier and said he'll bring us a proper meal a little later."

"So, you didn't discuss..." He stifled a yawn as he scooted toward the edge of the recliner.

"No. I thought whatever he had to say was something we both should hear. Which is why I asked him to come back."

Pushing himself up, he went to Riku's crib and looked down, expecting to see him sleeping. But Riku was wide awake, smiling. "Is he always happy in the morning?" he asked, turning to take the coffee.

"Always."

"Then he must get that from you because I hate mornings. Always have."

"Even when you were operating?"

"I functioned, and I made sure I was ready for it, but I didn't start my surgical schedule until eleven unless it was an emergency or I was overbooked. Came in around eight, caught up on charts for an hour, went on morning rounds with my residents, visited the family of my surgical patient, and by the time I'd done all that I was ready to operate. And, yes, you now know my deepest secret." He turned to Riku. "Your daddy doesn't do mornings very well, but I'll bet your mommy does."

"By this time, Riku and I are both ready to face the day, and if it's a nice morning we may already be back from a walk in the park. Oh, and I may have gotten in an hour of tutoring by now."

"Well, in my life now I'm already at work, Natalie has been yammering on about something I don't really care about for at least twenty minutes, and there are anywhere from three to five empty coffee cups on my desk." He walked over to the table next to Michi's recliner and selected a pastry—cream cheese. "Going out in the field isn't so bad. In fact, I like it, exploring old buildings or land. Those are the good days. The bad ones keep me at my desk or tie me up in meetings. I don't like being sedentary."

"Even with his condition and limitations, I try to make sure Riku isn't sedentary. Partly because he needs the mental stimulation but also because I'm preparing him for the future when he'll be able to resume normal activities…up to a point." She bent over the crib, rearranged a few tubes, and picked him up and simply held him to her chest. "When I was pregnant, and spending so much time in bed, I read every book I could on raising a baby. There are so many authorities, so many opinions. But in the end none of the so-called experts told you what to do if your child was sick. So, for me it's always been about using common sense."

"Maybe you should write a book," he suggested.

"Or we could, together. You from the medical perspective on raising a sick child, me from the emotional or mothering perspective."

"Which would suggest a relationship of some kind," he said, smiling. "Which means you'd write it then add my name as an afterthought?"

Michi blushed. "I suppose I deserve that, don't I?" She sat down in the rocker next to the crib, taking care not to jostle or loosen any of Riku's tubes or wires. She repositioned the oxygen cannula under his nose, and taped it back into place. "After what I've done."

Eric picked up a pineapple pastry and offered it to her, but she shook her head and looked down at Riku, as if he was the reason she couldn't or wouldn't eat. "Look, Michi, it's over. We can't go back. What I lost is lost, but I won't be put in that spot again. I won't allow it but, more than that, I don't believe you will allow it either. So from now on it's forward. No looking back. No anger. No guilt. None of that helps any of us."

"Why are you so kind to me?" she asked.

"Because that bundle in your arms is the best thing that's ever happened to me. We both created the mess…me with what you perceived me to be. And in some ways, my not sticking to anything for long does fit. Maybe not as much as you think. But it's what I projected, which is why I do understand why you weren't as keen to find me as you might have been otherwise."

"And my part of the mess?"

"Believing that you should tackle everything in life on your own. Independence is good, and I hope Riku gets that from you. But sometimes the struggles are too tough to face alone, and I don't think you know how to deal with that. Maybe you feel a little overshadowed because you come from such a strong family and you don't believe you measure up. Maybe your whole ordeal clouded your perspective a bit. I don't know what it is, but I do know that you're afraid to let a little of Riku go because the biggest fear you have is that in letting go you might also fail him. Or maybe someone else might see what you really fear."

"What do you mean, what I really fear?"

"I've spent a lot of hours trying to put together the pieces of your puzzle, Michi, and it all goes together except that one piece right in the middle. It's missing. And I think that's the piece, once put in place, that will finally tell me, and maybe even yourself, the real reason you're so protective."

"Because he's sick."

Eric shook his head. "Maybe that's what you're telling yourself, maybe that's what you even believe. But there's something else, Michi. Something you're not telling me, and maybe not even admitting to yourself."

"I wouldn't hurt him or do anything that would cause him any problems, Eric."

"Except maybe hide behind him?"

She blinked hard, then shut her eyes for a moment. "Is that what it looks like to you? That I hide behind him?" She opened her eyes slowly and look up at Eric. "Because I thought I put him before me. At least, I try to do that."

"And you do, Michi. Beautifully." He knelt beside the cradle and took Riku by the hand. Riku responded by giggling and squirming.

"I think he wants to be held by Daddy right now."

"Because he and Daddy swap stories. I tell him about all the mischief I got myself into when I wasn't much older than he is. And he tells me all the mischief he has planned for his future. Oh, and he really wants to learn how to play soccer. I was holding out for baseball, but Riku definitely prefers soccer."

Michi lifted him over to Eric, then stood to allow Eric to take the rocking chair. "I don't suppose I've ever heard Riku talk that much."

"He and I have this special language. You know, a father-son thing."

"Well, when he does start to talk, I can't even imagine the things he'll have to say since he takes it all in." Even now, Riku was fascinated watching the blue light on the cardiac monitor flash off and on.

Rather than cradling Riku the way Michi did, Eric sat him up more and let him lean into his own chest and thrash about a bit until he found his own comfortable spot. One where he could continue watching the machines. "Oh, and he wants a pony, just in case you didn't know that."

Michi laughed. "He told you that, too?"

"Well, not in so many words, but when I

asked him if he'd like a pony when he's a little older, his eyes sure lit up."

"You're going to spoil him, aren't you, Eric?"

"No. But I'm going to give him the kind of life my dad never gave me. And... I never had a pony."

"So, when do you buy him...?"

"Excuse me. I hate to interrupt," Henry said, 'but I've got some prep work to do before Riku's surgery tomorrow, as well as a long list of things my wife wants me to bring back from the city. So..."

"It's scheduled for tomorrow?" Michi asked, as her heart leapt to her throat.

"In the morning, first thing."

Her head started spinning, and her breaths were catching long before they reached her throat. "I suppose that's good," she said, looking down at Eric for support. "Eric?"

Eric nodded. "So, was there anything remarkably different on the last set of tests you took?"

"The overall picture is slightly less than it was before. Nothing to be alarmed about, but the gradual decline isn't going to stop. I did talk at length to Dr. Kapoor, who agrees we should go ahead with this. She'll be on her way back, but she doesn't want us to wait for her."

"So, this time tomorrow Riku will be…"

"In the middle of open-heart surgery," Henry said, stepping forward to take a pastry. "I'm on my way to Supply to make sure we have everything we'll need, and back-ups just in case. Then I'm going to have a look at the OR to familiarize myself with it. And after that, I've got to go in search of…" he pulled a hand-written list from his pocket, and read "'L'Amour de La Nuit Parisienne.'"

"She has good taste," Michi said. "Make sure you get the *eau de parfum* rather than the *eau de toilette*. Costs more, but worth it."

"You wouldn't happen to know what a *minaudière* is, would you? She wants one in black, with beads or crystals. But my question is one what?"

"It's a purse, Henry," Michi said. "There are

plenty of specialty handbag outlets in Manhattan, so look online."

"And I can find the perfume…?"

"At a perfumery. Again, look online for an address."

Henry chuckled. "We've been married thirty-three years and I still don't know what she's all about. But it's a good life." He looked at Eric, who was still holding a dozing Riku. "Especially if you can find a woman who knows what a *minaudière* is. Anyway, I've written a couple of orders for Riku, nothing drastic. And I'd like him to sleep as much as he can for the rest of the day. Both of you look like a nap might be in line as well." He held up his cellphone. "Call, text about any little thing. The last few hours leading up to the surgery are the toughest, so my suggestion would be to get yourself out of this room while he's sleeping, clear your head, and brace yourselves for tomorrow. It's going to be a rough day for both of you."

As if on cue, Takumi appeared in the room with a tray full of food. Various breads, fruits, yogurts, fresh juice. "Breakfast is served," he said, as Henry took a look at the abundance of food and shrugged. "If only I didn't have to go find that *minaudière*."

"Boutique Blanchfleur over on…" Takumi set the tray on the table then backed away. "Over near Godfrey Street and James Martin Circle."

"Well, it looks like my day is planned," Henry said, moving backwards toward the door. "So, like I said, call, text, whatever. And I'll let you know more later about the exact schedule for the morning."

Then he was gone. Takumi followed. And it was just the three of them again. A little family. Everything she'd ever wanted. Michi sat down in the recliner nearest Eric, kicked her footrest up, and sighed. Nothing was right in her world, yet the hopelessness she always lived with didn't seem as heavy right now. Even with tomorrow morning approaching faster than she wanted. "Do you mind if I close my eyes for a few minutes?" she asked.

Before Eric could respond, her eyes dropped shut, and her breathing evened out.

"You know you've got the best mommy in the world," he said to Riku, who was also nodding in and out. "So, it's up to the two of us now to figure out how to turn this into a real family."

He rocked Riku for a while longer, then put him back in the crib, sat down in the recliner next to Michi, and within just a few seconds all three of them were sleeping.

"I guess it was bad form having two sleeping doctors in the room while they were getting ready for their afternoon duties," Michi said, yawning and stretching as she leaned on the wall outside the door to Riku's room. "Or maybe we got kicked out because you were snoring too loudly." It was a little past noon now, and while a couple of hours of sleep didn't feel like much to most people, to Michi they were heaven sent. Two hours with no spotty waking every time Riku made a noise. Two hours away from her worries.

"You're the snorer," Eric said, standing next to her, stretching his muscles much the way a runner would do before a marathon. "Not me."

"Prove it," she challenged.

"How?"

She laughed. "You're the clever one. I'll leave that up to you."

"Let's see. The last person I slept with before sleeping with you in there was…you. So, will you be my witness?"

"I would except I don't sleep and tell. And I don't snore." She knew he was teasing her, and she enjoyed the lightness for a change. God knew, there hadn't been much of that in her life lately.

"Well, we might have to discuss this further in the future. But in the meantime, I need to go find someplace to take a shower, get myself in better shape or next time Riku wakes up he won't want to claim me."

"Actually, the stubble looks good. I like a man who's not quite clean-shaven."

"Then you must love me," he said, blushing immediately. "Not that I mean in love, but…"

"Don't worry about it," she said. "I know what you meant." Part of her wished he'd meant it differently, though.

She turned around to look at her reflection in the window to Riku's room and she looked pretty bad herself. Hair so mussed she wasn't sure it could ever be made right again. Wrinkled clothes. And while she wasn't actually slumping, it was an image that would have fit. "Well, maybe I could borrow some scrubs and find a shower somewhere myself."

"With me?" he teased, grinning at her.

"You wish." Smiling, Michi shook her head as she pushed herself off the wall and headed down the hall to the nurses' station to beg anything she could get to help her tidy up. Eric wasn't far behind, on the same mission, and when he stood next to her at the desk, waiting for the clerk to bring them soap, shampoo, towels and scrub uniforms, he was so close their arms touched.

It sent a shiver up her spine, and it surprised her that she could react to him so quickly. She had that night. But those had been different circumstances. And now…she wasn't prepared for this. The timing was so wrong. The situation so dire, yet even in the aftermath of something so innocent, she could still feel the shivers.

"I'd, um…" She shut her eyes, trying to get her mind back on track. "I'd thought about having the surgery done back home," she said, opening her eyes but avoiding looking into his. "I'm glad he's here, though. Glad that this time tomorrow he'll be through the worst of it."

"Why didn't you go through with it there?"

"Because of you. Even though I knew you couldn't be involved, I felt better knowing you were near."

"Would you have let him go into surgery without telling me?"

She shook her head. "I know you said no looking back, but for all I've done I wouldn't have done that. Not to either you or Riku. And I'm not lying to you, Eric. For everything I've done, I've never lied."

He took her hand in his as they waited. "I know that." Then he nudged into her a little harder and finally put his arm around her shoulder, pulling her against him. She didn't protest, didn't even try to move away, because she could feel his strength soaking into her pores. His was the strength she needed, even if she hadn't realized that until now.

Giving in to it even more, Michi leaned her head back against Eric's shoulder. "I'm so tired," she said on a sigh. "Too tired to think or move. Not even sure I've got enough left in me to breathe on my own. And this is something sleep won't fix. I'm glad you're here, and I'm glad we're not fighting."

He brought his other arm up and fully wrapped her into him. "I'm glad I'm here too, Michi. And that we're not fighting. But later, when everything has settled down, we really do need to figure this out. How I'm going to be involved in his life. Expectations that I have for him…and I do have them. There are a lot of things to straighten out when…"

She froze. Her body tensed, even though she didn't want it to. But the fears never totally went away, and when he talked about what he wanted, the floodgates always opened. It was a natural reaction. Especially now, after seeing how Eric was with Riku. But this was something she couldn't help. Something she couldn't overcome…at least, not yet. So, she pulled away from him. Or tried.

But Eric wouldn't let her go. He held onto her, perhaps because he needed the feel of her almost as much as she needed the feel of him. "He's going back to Sapporo when he's better, Eric," she said, her voice so tentative she barely recognized it. "To his home. That's always been the plan. He needs to be there…in a place he knows."

"As he should. I'm not taking him from you, Michi, and I don't know what it will take for me to convince you that I want what's best for both of you. I'm not looking for custody. Not looking to infringe in any way. But I do want my place in his life and I think we both need to figure out how that's going to happen."

"I don't want to be on the defensive," she said. "Always scared that something will happen, that someone will try to take him from me."

"You mean me?"

She nodded. "And the social workers at the hospital." She stepped away from the desk, then walked down the hall to a private consultation room. Eric followed her in and shut the door. He led her to a chair and she sat, but only on the edge. "That other piece of the puzzle… it comes back to haunt me in so many ways. And maybe I should have told you sooner, but this isn't easy to talk about."

"If you can't, then…"

"No, I have to. My sins are never about lying but always about omission. You need to know what drives my constant fear that someone will take Riku from me." She shut her eyes for a moment, as if she was trying to convince herself to go on. This was very difficult for her. It showed on her body, in her face, in the way she wrung her hands.

"Take your time," he said gently.

"That's one of the problems. I've already taken too much time." She let out a long, weary sigh. "And please, after you hear what I say, don't judge me. I've already done enough of that for the two of us."

"What is it, Michi?"

"They thought I wasn't fit. That somehow my lifestyle during my pregnancy had caused his heart defect."

"What?"

"They accused me of taking drugs."

"Who?"

"The social workers at the hospital."

Eric blinked hard. "But you were sick. How could these people..." He balled his hands into fists. "I don't understand."

"I took blood thinner shots. They're approved for pregnancy, very safe, and clotting was a huge concern for me right from the start. Three times before, when I've tried to have a baby, I've thrown a clot that terminated the pregnancy. So, for me the shots were vital once I knew I was pregnant."

"But how did the social workers...and at your parents' hospital. Didn't they know you?"

"I wasn't going through anybody at my parents' hospital. I was going someplace where nobody knew me, afraid that if people knew what I'd done, it would bring shame to my parents. And before you say anything, yes, that's an old way. Very traditional, but I respect my parents' sense of tradition. People aren't so concerned about those things any more. But I was trying to save face, so I went elsewhere."

"Still, the jump from blood thinner to drugs…how?"

"I taught one more seminar after you left. I was very early into pregnancy, not really unwell but experiencing the usual things. Morning sickness, vomiting. Anyway, one of my students, a social worker in the hospital where I was going for care, caught me retching in the bathroom and made the off-handed comment that the first trimester was the worst. So far I hadn't told anybody I was pregnant, but since she'd already guessed, we talked about it for a bit. Nothing serious. Mostly about the four children she'd had, and her morning sickness, how many hours of labor, that sort of thing. And as it was the last day of the seminar and

I knew I'd never see her again, I didn't mind opening up. She seemed very nice.

"Anyway, later I went to take my shot, and she walked in. I didn't think anything of it. You know, hike up the shirt, swab the belly, take the shot. She asked if I was diabetic, and I told her no. Since my condition was none of her business, I didn't say anything else, which left her believing I was…taking some kind of drug."

"OK, that makes a little sense. Not much, but I can understand how someone who works in the medical system but who isn't medical could get confused. But how did it progress to the point where you were being called unfit?"

Michi shook her head. "Because I told her who I was seeing when we had that chat, she called my doctor and reported what she'd seen…me shooting up drugs. Except my doctor was off on holiday, so one of the associates took the call and simply filed the paperwork to put me under investigation. Nobody even asked me, Eric. I swear… I had no idea all this was going on.

"So, when my condition started to go bad, my own doctor hospitalized me for some tests, and I suppose my admittance sent up some kind of red flag. Another social worker came, told me she'd been advised that I was potentially harming my baby, and you can guess the rest. For a little while I was put in protective custody, pending further investigation. Literally arrested and charged with a crime. And later, even though my doctor straightened it out, and the arrest was erased from the books, the red flag never came down and I lived under this scrutiny, and stigma.

"I realize they were doing what they thought best, but there I was, fighting to keep my child, getting sicker and sicker, and the whole suspicion that I could be causing my problems… I was labeled as having Munchausen syndrome, Eric. You know, where I was hurting myself, or by proxy hurting my unborn child, to get attention. And I was mandated for psychiatric counseling."

"That's ridiculous. How can taking a blood thinner elevate to psychiatric counseling?"

"It was wrong, but it happened. And my psychiatrist, once she understood the situation, was fighting for me. But once the word is whispered, you can't take it back. I was being called a threat to my unborn child, and it was only after I finally told my dad what was happening that he stepped in and, well, long story short, I spent the rest of my pregnancy in his hospital, under the care of another high-risk obstetrician. But it all came back when Riku was born sick. The threats to take him from me. To declare me unfit to be a mother.

"Words, Eric. Once they're spoken you can't un-speak them. Accusations are the same way. Once they're made, if people believe them, they're not inclined to be talked out of what they think they know."

"And you couldn't tell me this?"

"I couldn't. Even now, aren't you wondering if what they said is true? There were so many problems with me, with Riku... Don't I look like I could be complicit in some way?"

"No!" he said, fighting to remain calm. "That's not you."

"Even after I made a rather controversial decision to delay his surgery when, traditionally, it's done when the child is much younger?"

"Under your doctor's advisement, Michi."

"My family and all my doctors stood behind me, Eric. But one person who misunderstood something she saw almost cost me my son. It was a tiny, tiny snowball that avalanched. And because I'd lost pregnancies in the past, all I knew was that I had to withdraw from everything to give Riku a fighting chance to get into the world. So, while I was being threatened, and even watched, I simply shut my eyes to everything, including you, and the only thing I allowed in my mind was my baby. So, it's not fierce independence you saw as much as abject fear. And it damaged me. I don't trust. I'm always afraid that something I'll do will cause more problems."

"Are you getting help, Michi?" he asked, kneeling next to her and taking her hand.

"I have. And I will again when I go back home. But the stigma of it all, Eric… I can't deal with it and be there for Riku. I know I overcompensate by being protective, but what if I take him out on a chilly day, and someone thinks he's not dressed warmly enough? Or what if they see him without his oxygen and don't know he's allowed to be off it from time to time?" She swatted back tears.

"What if I came here and told you that you have a son you never knew about, that he's sick, that I went against traditional advice on when the surgery should be done and did what I believed to be right? Maybe to you it would make sense. But to someone else like the social worker who saw me take my blood thinner and had me arrested for it? That's why I'm scared all the time, Eric. They labeled me with a syndrome I don't have, accused me of things I didn't do and I'm always afraid that there's going to be a third round, and this one I'll lose."

"I wish I'd known," he said.

"Then what? You'd start watching me, too?"

"I don't even know what to say because if I didn't know you, I might have. Or you might have, if you suspected abuse in one of your patients." He sighed heavily. "I'm so sorry. But you're not in this alone. None of it. And for what it's worth, I know there's nothing about you that's unfit. I trust that, Michi. Trust it and believe it. And I'll go to the mat for you if that's what I have to do to make it right."

"Thank you," she said, then leaned forward and fell into his arms and sobbed. And for the next half-hour neither of them spoke. There were no words to say. Only emotion, and deep, deep pain. For both of them.

"Do you think they've had enough time to get everything set for the afternoon?" she asked, knowing her face was swollen now, which would only make her look worse than she had before. "I need to hold him. Or sit next to him. Whatever he's up to tolerating."

"Let's give them a few more minutes. The nurses here are thorough. They're going to take care of Riku the way you would. And it's only been a little over half an hour."

Thirty-plus minutes that seemed like forever. Like when she was a child and one of her parents would tell her to wait a few minutes for something—to open a gift or have a piece of birthday cake. So much of that little girl was still in her—the one who was always impatient to make things happen. Probably because everything behind her now still scared her and her only hope was going forward as fast as she could to get away from it.

"When I was a little girl, I always knew I was going to grow up to be a doctor. It was the life I lived because of my parents, the only life I knew. And even when I was young, I understood how what they did was important. Sometimes one or the other would take me to work with them, and I'd see all the looks of admiration people would give them. It made me proud to be their daughter, to be part of something that made such a huge difference in the lives of so many people.

"So that was always set for me. There was never a time that I didn't want to be a doctor."

"Was being a physiatrist something you always wanted?" he asked.

Michi laughed. "No. That came when I was

in medical school, and I saw the difference that could be made in a group of people who might not have anywhere else to turn. Part of our practice deals with helping people overcome the disabilities they've received from strokes or accidents. Apart from the therapy they need, we offer them lifestyle, and changes that can make an overall difference in quality-of-life issues. So maybe we can't get someone out of a wheelchair, but we can teach them to live their life to the fullest with their other capabilities.

"Modern medicine doesn't always know what to do with those who don't make a full recovery but recover enough to get back to life. So, when I saw that happening, I knew that was what I wanted to do. For me, it's exciting knowing I can be part of something so life-changing, so important."

"But there are medical consequences, aren't there?"

"Of course there are. The people who come to me are injured or physically broken. They need modern medicine to help them get along.

Therapy, medications…you name it. In my case, I specialize in athletes. One of my partners is all about stroke recovery. Another is about degenerative disease processes like arthritis and neuro-muscular diseases. We have a pediatric specialist, who will work with Riku when the time comes, and someone who specializes in teenagers."

She paused and smiled. There were times when she thought she'd moved so far away from her world that she'd never get back to it, not fully. But something about Eric gave her optimism, and she truly hoped he could find his way back to his real world as well. That was where he was happiest and she did so want him to be happy. "People survive injuries and conditions that not so long ago would have killed them. My job, as a doctor, is to teach them how to survive through any means we have available."

"You wouldn't have had the patience to be a surgeon, would you?"

She laughed. "You noticed that in me? Because you're right. I like results I can see and patients I can form a long-term bond with. As a surgeon, you don't get to have that. Your patients get fixed, and you're only allowed to see the tip of the iceberg with that. Sure, you may have follow-up appointments, but those don't last long. And your bond is only for that short period of time that child is your patient. Then there's another child, another temporary bond.

"My patients stay. And I like that because I love watching progress over the long term. So, no, I couldn't have done what you did. You save a child and you take the front spot as the hero. I teach a patient with ankylosing spondylitis a better way to sleep to give him pain relief over the long term, and there's no one in the hall outside their hospital room giving me a hero's accolades. But that's OK because if my patient does sleep better because of me, I'm happy."

"Well, your seminar was an eye-opener for me. I was actually considering bringing a physiatrist into my practice for a little while. I'd even decided to talk to you about coming over to set it up for me. But we all know how that turned out, don't we?"

"Unfortunately," she said, smiling as she thought of Riku getting to the point where physiatry would benefit him. She'd never thought that far ahead before. But now the future was creeping in and she didn't want to stop it.

"So, his name. Why did you decide on Riku?"

"First, because it's a traditional name. Depending on how it's spelled in Japanese, it can mean several things. The way I spell it, it means enduring for a long time. I suppose I needed that reassurance, given the difficulties he had at birth."

"Does he have another name?"

"Like what you would consider a middle name? You do know that in Japan we don't use middle names. Even our documents such as passports and family registries have no place to write a middle name. But because Riku is half-yours, out of respect for your culture I did give him a middle name. It's Haru, spelled to mean eternal treasure. Because that's what he is. My eternal treasure."

"Riku Haru… Sato?"

"Yes, Sato."

"It's strong. The way he will be after his surgeries."

"I'm surprised you don't want to get your name in there somewhere. Isn't that a tradition, to give the firstborn son part or all of the father's name?"

"It is, and I'm actually the fourth Eric Alexander Hart in line. And, no, Riku doesn't need my name. There's no thought to it. And his name…it's all about thought and love. It's a good name, Michi. A very good name."

She was glad, because for a little while she'd thought about calling Riku Eric. But that had changed when she'd first set eyes on her baby and had known he needed something from her tradition. Something that would give him a strong identity later in his life. And to her, his name promised a life beyond his illness.

"I really do need to get back to him," she said, twisting in Eric's arms to pull herself away from him. As she pushed away, though, a tingle of dizziness washed over her, probably from worry or a lack of sleep or eating. She wasn't worried, because whatever had caused it would go away once she was back sitting next to Riku's bed. But another step brought on even more spinning, and Michi reached out to Eric to take hold of his arm to steady himself. "Maybe I should have eaten something after all," she said, shutting her eyes to let the wobbly floor around her settle down. "One of those pastries earlier."

"Michi, are you OK?" Eric took a firm hold of her arm and held tight as she reached for the wall to hold herself up.

But the tightness in her chest was barely allowing her to breathe. "Just tired," she said, trying to regain her bearings. "I wasn't expecting any of this. Even though I knew the surgery had to happen, I never really admitted it to myself, and now that it's so close…" She went to turn around but instead staggered into him. "Maybe after we're sure Riku's going to be OK, you can sit with him while I go find something to eat." His gentle hand on her arm caused another shiver, but this time it was from the awareness of how close they were standing, of how she could hear his every breath and almost feel the beat of his heart.

"Maybe I should carry you," he said, his voice so low it nearly blended with the night.

"You offered to do that once before. Remember?" Their night together, when he'd offered to carry her to his room. It had been a romantic gesture, but as unnecessary then as it was now. "But, no, I don't want to be carried. I'm perfectly capable of getting there on my own." Yet maybe with some of his help. "I may be a little dizzy, but it's nothing that requires a knight in shining armor to come to the rescue. I just need to go back to Riku. Make sure his favorite teddy bear is tucked in bed with him."

He nudged her chin up with his thumb. "What you need is to follow doctor's orders, and this doctor is prescribing a knight in shining armor, even if only for a little while. You need someone to take care of you so that when he needs you, you're up to taking care of Riku."

"But I don't want to be carried," she said, looking into his eyes. "No one's ever had to do that for me, and now's not the time to see if what happens in the romance novels really works. You know, the hero whisks her into his arms, carries her off, and all is well. That's not my story, Eric. Mine's where I do everything I can to get from day to day. That's the way it's been for a long time now."

"Maybe you don't need someone to carry you in the literal sense," he continued, "but in the sense that even *you* need to give in and let someone take care of you from time to time."

"Even after what I've done to you?"

"Even after what you've done to me. But also, even after what's been done to you. Your needs count, Michi. You've taken so much of the bad for so long I think you may have forgotten there's good out there for you, too."

"It is. My parents, my brother...the rest of my family."

"I'm part of that family, you know. Maybe

not in the way most people would consider it. But we all have one thing in common…wanting the best for Riku. And for you. And if that means me having to pick you up and throw you over my shoulder…"

Michi stepped back from the door then turned to face him, stood on her toes and kissed him on the cheek. "Thank you for listening," she said. "And caring. You make things easier."

His gaze locked in on Michi's face, taking in the vulnerability in her eyes, the fear in her face. "I hope to make them better as well," he said, realizing he was as caught in her spell as he had been that one night they'd had together. He'd wanted her like he'd wanted no other woman before, and no one had come close to filling that need in him after her. Her intellect, her determination, her sense of duty…and her beauty. One look at her had told him he was way out of her league. Women like that didn't happen in his life, so he'd walked away from it with regrets, knowing it was only a fantasy. This time he wasn't walking away from it.

"Michi," he said, as she turned away to finally leave. "What about you? Do you want to work on making things better between us... not just for Riku but for us?"

"I do, but..."

"But you still don't trust me enough?"

She shook her head. "No, I do trust you. But I don't want to be divided. Not right now. Not when Riku needs all of me." She brushed her hand across his cheek. "Everything is so tentative, and I'm just...just not in that space. But I want to be, Eric. I promise, I want to be, and I hope you'll be patient with me for a while because, right now, Riku comes first."

"I understand," he said, helpless to back away from her, from them... But her words gave him hope, and that was all he needed for now. A little hope, a vision of the future filling him with desires and wild thoughts of things he'd never imagined for himself. So, with a gentle hold, he cupped the back of her neck and kissed her deeply, possessive in his touch yet still tentative.

Was this taking advantage of her now that

she was so defenseless because of a situation neither of them could control? Or did she need his toughness the way he needed hers? "Should we stop?" he asked, twining his fingers through her silky hair.

She didn't answer right away, which he feared *was* her answer. But then suddenly Michi's body melded to his with an answering moan, and she offered up her mouth in a ravaging need he understood. Desire overtook him with a searing shudder, then took hold of his conscience. And it felt like a dagger piercing his heart when common sense finally returned, and he gripped her arms and pushed her back, his breaths so labored he feared he would be overtaken by lightheadedness.

"As much as I hate to say this, we can't do this because neither one of us can know what it is. Not in a real sense." He dropped his hold on her and stepped back. "And trust me, if circumstances were different, I wouldn't be walking away from this. Not this time. But we've got to take it slowly right now, to see what's there after Riku has recovered. Anything else could hurt all three of us. So, I'm sorry, Michi. I should never have started this. Will you forgive me?"

"I did before," she said, then turned away from him and finally left the waiting room. Her steps down the hall, as he watched from the doorway, were slow, though. And he wondered if he'd made her cry. God help him, that was the last thing he'd wanted to do.

CHAPTER EIGHT

THE DAY DRAGGED BY with surgical prep and adjustments to the various equipment and tubes Riku was hooked to. Michi spent a good bit of the rest of the day with her family, especially her parents, who'd flown in from Japan, while he caught up on work, not going into the office but doing it by phone. Then the night turned into one of the longest of his life. Maybe even *the* longest.

Riku was sleeping soundly now, and even though it was early, he and Michi took to their respective recliner chairs, made themselves comfortable, and didn't sleep. He'd offered to split the night with her, staying awake for half of it while she slept, then switching around. But she'd declined, claiming she was too wound up to sleep.

Truth was, he was wound pretty tight himself. So, there they'd sat, hour upon hour, quietly, so as not to waken Riku. He'd stared at the ceiling most of the time. And whenever he'd glanced over at Michi, she'd been watching Riku. He wanted to talk to her, or hold her or do something, but she wasn't going to leave Riku's side, and to stay there meant being extra quiet.

Once, when Riku stirred and set off an alarm, they both practically jumped to get to his bedside, but she was faster. More practice, he supposed. Thankfully, it was nothing. Riku had tried turning, causing one of his wires to come loose, tangling his chubby little fist in it. Michi took care of it, of course, then settled back into her chair once Riku had gone to sleep again.

"Am I of any use here?" he whispered.

"It's nice to have someone to back me up," she said. "Makes me feel less alone. And I think he needs you to be here. But if you have other things to do…"

"No, everything's under control," he said, hoping that was the case. Right now, the corporate part of his life was so distant, so unimportant he didn't even want to think about it. And for all the good his afternoon efforts had been toward answering correspondence and emails, after Natalie had brought him his computer, he simply wasn't in the mood.

Here he was with all the money anyone could ever hope for, and all the resources, but none of that was doing Riku any good. It was funny how his dad had always counted on money as the means to fix everything, yet what was required now was a skill he had but couldn't use. It made him feel so damned helpless. "But if you don't mind, I'm going to go stretch my legs. Can I bring you anything?" he asked on his way to the hall. He was restless. Needed some space. Time to think. Early morning activity had already picked up in the hall the same way it had the day before. Doctors were making rounds, nurses were getting patients up and started for the day, parents who'd stayed over were emerging from patient rooms or wherever they'd slept, looking for coffee.

Soon they would come for Riku. That was what scared him more than he cared to admit. And even though he knew the procedure step by step, that didn't settle him.

"I'm good," she whispered, not taking her eyes off Riku. "Maybe after they take him in, I'll go get something, perhaps leave the hospital for a bit to clear my head. I'm not sure I can be here while…"

She was feeling the things he was at the moment. Fear, anxiety, the need to grab Riku and run someplace far from here where he would be safe and happy and healthy. "Just text me if you hear anything."

She nodded then shut her eyes, retreating into a world where children didn't need surgery and parents lived happily ever after.

Eric had been gone an hour now, and while she wasn't worried about it, she did wonder when he was coming back. As the minutes ticked off the clock, and Riku was getting closer and closer to the surgery, she was finding herself so edgy she couldn't concentrate. More than that, she'd begun doubting every little thing she did. Even changing Riku's diaper had set her off in a panic because if things didn't go as planned, and if the unspeakable did happen, something as simple as a diaper change would hold such incredibly strong memories. And not good ones.

Michi desperately wanted her memories to be good. Part of those memories included Eric and how amazing he was with Riku. He was a natural. His instincts were perfect, and not only because he'd chosen a career helping sick children. His instincts were the right ones for being a great dad.

And he was being so good to her, too. Even though he had every right to be angry, and even hate her. In fact, he was so good, now she was thinking about Eric, there were tears running down her cheeks for all the things they might have been, and all the things she'd done to make sure none of that would ever happen.

"Why?" she whispered, as she watched her son. "Why am I so afraid of letting him in?"

Once she'd believed it was because he might

take Riku from her if he believed her unfit. But he didn't, and he had proved that over and over. Even after she'd told him how they'd tried to claim she was trying to harm her baby even before he was born, Eric didn't believe that. He hadn't even come close to believing it.

So, what was it she was feeling, that constant undertow of something trying to drag her along, trying to get her from place to place? Could her feelings for Eric be deeper than she'd intended to allow? Not just caring for him as Riku's father but perhaps falling a little in love herself? It wasn't out of the question and there were times the urge was so strong it almost overtook her. Admittedly, her timing was bad. But not her intention.

Michi stood, then leaned over the rails of the crib to straighten Riku's blankets and check to make sure he was doing as well as could be expected. The monitors everywhere told her he was, but she had to touch him, feel his soft skin, lay her hand across his chest for a moment to feel the rise and fall of it. To love someone this much scared her. It had scared her from the moment she'd known she was carrying him. Because love was such a huge responsibility, and there were so many ways to let someone down inside it.

Tears streaked down her cheeks again, but as she stepped away from the crib, she stepped backwards into Eric's arms. And he held her, and let her cry quietly on his shoulder for what seemed an eternity. Her body was racked with sobs, but she didn't want to move, couldn't move, and for the first time in so long she couldn't even remember she felt a faint glimmer of hope that everything would be fine.

"I'm sorry," she whispered, sniffling. "I don't usually cry this much. But with everything that's going on, it's like I can't turn it off."

He handed her a tissue and led her away from the crib. But not too far away because he understood her need to be there. "It gets overwhelming sometimes," she said. "And frustrating, with all this waiting." He was still holding her, but not as tightly. And she liked being where she was. Eric made things right. Feeling his physical presence, knowing that no matter what she'd done she had his support…

"And while everybody in my family is so supportive, they haven't been through anything like this, so they can't fully understand. And sometimes I feel so alone I don't know what to do. Sometimes I'd like to be weak for a little while, so I can turn my pain over to someone else for a few minutes until I can regroup and start it all over again." She sniffled. "Being independent isn't always so easy, you know."

"Why try so hard at it?"

"Because I've invested so much into my work I've let the whole personal side of my life go. Meeting you, then having that night… that was the first time I ever let myself go, Eric, and simply enjoy something—you— because I wanted to. I've always felt like I had to compete with my entire family to be as successful as they are. And sometimes that was just so difficult. I've always felt insignificant when everything else around me exuded success. Then when they accused me of Munchausen's, even though I knew they were wrong, I doubted myself. Not in that I'd ever do anything to harm my baby, because I wouldn't. But I wondered what kind of outward appearance I projected that would make people think of me in such a way."

"That was the pressure getting to you, Michi, the pressure you put on yourself. The people who know you don't see the things in you that you see."

"There was always a lot of pressure on me to uphold the family reputation," she conceded. "My parents are wonderful, don't get me wrong. But look at them. Look at what they've done together. Growing up knowing the same is expected of you isn't easy, which is why I've always kept to myself, for fear I'd be called out as a fraud. And here, in this crib, is the proof of that. As much as I've loved him from the start, I was doubted. My love was doubted. My need to protect my baby was doubted.

"I love my career, Eric. Love building my clinic. But I also love being a mother more than anything, and when I look at Riku I'm aware that everything I've built myself to be is just a façade. The only thing that matters is my son. And without him…who am I?"

"You're who you always were, Michi. Riku doesn't change that. In fact, when we were together in Japan I didn't even consider that you were truly approachable. You held yourself back. I knew there was more, could almost see it surface, but you didn't let it. And now, as I see you with Riku, I see that same bright, hard-working woman, but through a gentler focus. Riku brings out the best in you and I don't think you ever had that opportunity before because you were so busy trying to be the person you believed your family wanted you to be. As Shakespeare's Polonius said, *'To thine own self be true.'* I think this is the first time you're allowing yourself to do that."

"Well, it's not easy."

He chuckled. "It gets easier with help."

She reached up and stroked his cheek. "You're such a good man, Eric. You didn't deserve a disaster like me in your life."

"But without you I wouldn't have Riku. And I'll admit it was love at first sight with him." Maybe with her, too. Definitely a little. But maybe more than he was ready to admit. "So, can you tell me about him?" Eric laughed. "You promised to, but we didn't get around to it. We can stand in the hall just to get you out of the room for a while, but you can still see him, if that's what you'd prefer. Or we can do anything or go anyplace as long as you tell me about Riku. I need to know more about my son before his surgery. You know…what makes him laugh besides giraffes? What piques his interest? What he doesn't like other than radishes. What is he like?"

She followed Eric to the door of the hospital room, then stepped out and found the place where everything in the entire room was visible to her. "First, he's always happy. He laughs and smiles all the time. Even when he's sick sometimes. It's like he knows that's what he was put here on earth to be and he tries his best to do it. Also, besides *your* studious look, which he gets when he's trying to figure out something new to him, he also has your smile. And when he's feeling good, he's very vocal, not so much in words as in sounds."

She smiled. "But he understands what I say, because he's smart, Eric. Sometimes it's hard to see it because so often he doesn't feel well, but on his good days I love watching how methodical he is. He's definitely going to grow up to be a thinker like you."

"Well, for sure, he's a fighter. Like you, Michi. I've watched him play, watched the way he deals with all these things attached to him now, and he fights his way through, meaning he's one tough little kid. Tough, like his mom."

"Is that a good thing?" she asked.

"It's called determination and, yes, it's a very good thing."

"Then maybe he's the best of both of us." She stepped inside the door a little more, then held out her hand to Eric. "Look at him." she said, as Eric took her hand and stepped to her side. "He's not asleep. He's studying the cardiac monitor. I wonder what his two-year-old mind is thinking about it?"

"How to take it apart and put it back together, probably." He chuckled. "Like me, in surgery."

"Then maybe he'll be a surgeon."

"Or an engineer. Or a mechanic. Or anything he wants to be."

Eric's unbridled enthusiasm filled her with so much hope for Riku's future. This was the first time she'd ever really allowed herself to feel optimistic about his future, and she owed this to Eric. Where all she saw was illness, all he saw was potential. Which made her happy beyond belief.

"I want him to get better so badly, and I can visualize all the things we'll do, but sometimes it's so hard to see it. Sometimes those images just aren't in my head, which makes me feel like I'm letting him down." This was the first time she'd ever said that to anyone. But it was true. Her inability to always see a bright future ahead made her feel like she was a bad mother.

Eric slipped his arm around her waist—something that had become so normal for them. "In a sense, his illness has also become his normal. You expect that, and you anticipate all the things that could happen as a result. But thinking in other terms, terms that have nothing to do with his heart, frightens you because you're not prepared to go off in another direction, or deal with something else that might come up. You're afraid you can't handle that. Like including his father in his life."

She nodded. "It's been easier to avoid the things that scare me rather than face them head on, and what I thought you might do scared me."

"Even now?" he asked.

Before she could answer, the heart monitor alarm went off, and Michi and Eric ran to his bedside. Eric studied the rhythm tracing across the monitor screen while Michi repositioned Riku for better access to his chest. Then they were pushed away from the room as several nurses and a couple of doctors rushed in.

"This has been my life, Eric. Complications,

over and over. I can't…" She choked, then cleared her throat. "I can't keep on doing this. Not for Riku's sake, not for my own. Being strong… I can't even pretend any longer." She looked up at him as they walked to the waiting room at the end of the hall…the one where her family wasn't gathered. The one where they could be alone.

"You don't have to pretend anything, Michi. The people who matter know who you are and what you're going through. All the support you want is there when you need it. And here…" He opened his arms to her. "For the rest of your life."

She fell into his open arms and stayed there, letting him hold her, loving his comfort. Loving him. Until there was a knock at the door and Henry's entrance signaled the beginning of the next phase.

"It's time," Henry said. "Everything's ready, the OR is prepped, I have a good surgical team, and Dr. Kapoor is on her way, even though she won't get here in time. So…"

"How long?" Eric asked.

"Inside the hour. But you still have some time to be with him before we take him down to surgery."

Michi swallowed hard. Looked at Eric, who had tears in his eyes. Then she looked into the faces of her family, who'd followed Henry to find them, but didn't see in any of them what she saw in Eric—a love greater than anything she'd ever seen before.

"I'd like to scrub in, Henry. If that's all right with you. Just to be with Riku. That's all."

Henry nodded, then smiled. "I never assumed you wouldn't."

Then the furor began. People everywhere in Riku's room, doing various jobs. Changing his clothes, adjusting his medicines, removing old wires and replacing them with new ones. More leads on his chest. Medication adjustments. In the hall outside, Michi and Eric watched as ten people surrounded Riku's bed, practically swallowing him up in all the activity. And all she wanted was to hold him. "I'm glad you're going in with him," she said. "He needs you there."

"There's nothing I can really do, but it felt like I had to be there anyway."

"Because you're a surgeon, Eric." She looked up at him. "That hasn't changed. And I hope you realize that before you're gone from it so long you can't go back."

"Do you think I'll go back?" he asked her.

"I think that once we're through this and Riku is recovering nicely, you'll have an overwhelming need to stay close to the things that make you happiest in life. At least, that's what I'm hoping for myself. And I think we're a lot alike in that. If surgery is what makes you happiest…"

Choosing what made him happiest. Becoming a doctor might have been the only time he'd ever done that. In a way, it was an odd concept but a good one.

"*Medice, cura te ipsum,*" Eric said. *Physician, heal thyself.* A saying from a Greek proverb.

His whole body ached because he'd probably slept badly in a chair much too small for him, but he was doing what he always did before he performed a procedure…he called it warming up his surgeon's mind. Going over, in his head, the procedure. Step by step. Looking at it from every angle, anticipating the problems, listing all the things that could go wrong and gearing up to correct them if they did. Here, in his pre-surgery shower, that was what he always did, and even though he had no authority in the OR this time, the habit was still there.

"I could, um…after the surgery is over and we get into that waiting phase of recovery," Michi said, mustering all the optimism she could, now that the surgery was mere minutes away, "I could stay awake and wait if you need to take a nap. You look exhausted."

"Probably because I am," he said, from the shower. He was inside, while she was standing outside, leaning on the wall, waiting for him to emerge.

"But you'll be okay to be in surgery with him?" The room was steamy and warm, but not too warm that she was working up a sweat, as all she could feel now was the stark, cold chill of fear.

"I'll be fine," he said, finally stepping out, bare-chested, barefoot, with a towel wrapped around his middle.

He was a good-looking man, she thought. Even now, when everything she had was focused on Riku, she did take a moment to admire what she had in front of her. The memory had always been vivid. Eric was as beautiful physically as any man she'd ever seen. Now, and then. "But if you start to get too tired…" she said, as he grabbed a pair of clean scrubs off the hook near the shower and began to drop his towel to the floor.

Even though he wasn't modest, hadn't been that night, didn't seem to be now, she spun around to allow him a modicum of privacy, and to allow herself to think about something other than the physical man.

Eric chuckled. "We made a baby together. You don't have to be shy."

"Well, you're certainly not. But I… I need to keep my thoughts focused on Riku."

"And I would distract you?"

"Everything would distract me, Eric. Right now, I don't want to think about what I have to think about, and any distraction will do. Which is why I can't be distracted."

"But I'm not just any distraction, Michi." He took hold of her shoulder and pulled her around straight into his arms, straight into his bare chest, where she buried her head and shut her eyes. Thankfully, his scrub pants were on, but his feet were still bare, and his hair dripped water down the side of her face. "We're going to get through this," he said, holding her tight. "And on the other side, when Riku's better, we'll figure out what we are, and who we are."

She looked up at him. "It's like I'm not even here, Eric. I am, yet I'm someplace else where none of this is necessary. If something happens in there, if there are decisions…you do that, Eric. Please, do what's right for Riku. I've already told Henry to allow you to make the decisions, if that becomes necessary."

"Why?" he asked, his voice thick.

"Because this is what you do, who you are.

Because I trust you with your son's life. Because I believe you would trade places with him if you could."

"I would," he said. "I would take his place in a heartbeat…"

"Which is why I trust you with his life. His life is part of your life now, and you'll do the right thing." She stepped back, grabbed the scrub shirt from the hook on the wall and handed it to him. "And I believe surgery generally requires shoes, too." She braved a smile that lasted mere seconds, then disappeared.

Deep in her heart she truly did know Eric loved Riku. It wasn't the kind of love that came of getting to know someone, or a love born of familiarity. It was the love of a parent. The same love she felt. And her heart skipped a beat when she realized this. Eric was such a good man. Easy to love. And she'd already fallen. So many ways to love. Her life was blessed with them. "So, you'd better get them on and get out there. The most important person in your life needs his daddy now."

Michi turned away immediately, trying to

regain control. But that wasn't going to happen until Eric came out of surgery and told her himself that Riku had come through like a champ. "Take care of him in there," she said, on her way to the door. "Take care of our son, Eric."

Then she stepped into the hall, looked right and left for someplace to go to have the good, hard cry she needed before she walked the hall to surgery holding her son's hand. As it turned out, that cry came in an empty utility closet just outside the hall to the suite of operating rooms. And there she sobbed until her throat hurt and her eyes were swollen. Ten minutes later, when she stepped into the hall, Eric was standing there with a tissue and a bottle of water for her. Smiling, not questioning.

"It's time," was all he said. Then he took her hand and led her back to Riku's room, now vacated by all the techs and nurses, where Riku was already getting groggy from his pre-surgery IV induction of a medicine that would have him well asleep even before he got to the OR.

Then came the surgical nurses, ready to move him. So Michi took hold of Riku's right hand, while Eric took hold of his left and, for the first time, they walked together as a family of three. Riku in his bed, with his parents on either side while he slept, unaware that his world was about to be changed drastically.

All too soon, they were at the surgery entrance where Eric would go on with Riku and she would go to her parents to wait. "Mommy loves you," she said, bending down to kiss him. "And when you wake up, she'll be right there with you."

Eric didn't say a word as they pushed through the doors and left Michi behind, standing at the window, looking in as he and Riku turned the corner to the operating room assigned to Riku's surgery. He took one look over his shoulder as he turned that corner, and tried to manage a supportive smile for Michi. Then he went to the scrub room for that part of the prep, while Riku was wheeled into the actual operating room.

And Michi… She'd made it mere steps

away from the door when she gave out, leaned against the wall and slid silently to the floor. Not crying. Not reacting. Not…anything. Too numb. That was where Agnes found her and helped her to a private waiting room and into the arms of her family.

But it was Eric's arms she needed. And it was in Eric's arms she'd be when this day was over and Riku was asleep, and closer to being healthy than he'd ever been before. Her little family. That was what she wanted them to be. And it became part of the dream of her heart. Eric and Riku and her together…all of them healthy and safe. And so loved. That was the full dream of her heart now. The only one.

The clock simply wouldn't move. It seemed like every time she looked up it, it was at the same place it had been the time before. How long had it been so far? Over three hours?

"He's good," Eric assured her. He'd left the OR when Dr. Kapoor had arrived to assist, and the OR had got too crowded. "These things take time, and you can't always predict what's going to come up along the way. But that doesn't mean anything's wrong." They were alone again. She'd sat with her parents for the first two hours but in their worry they'd seemed...clingy. She didn't want clingy. Wasn't able to tolerate it, even from her family.

So, she'd returned to the private waiting room where she and Eric had talked hours ago and shut herself in, wanting to hide herself away from everything. Eric had joined her only moments later, making her realize it wasn't being alone that she wanted. It was being with Eric that meant everything.

"And nothing's going wrong?"

"You've got Henry and Anjali in there. The best tag team in the world, in my opinion. They're not going to miss anything, Michi. They're not going to let anything happen."

"I wish it could be you," she said.

"If you mean on the table, with my chest cracked, so do I. If you mean performing the surgery..." He held out his shaky hands. "Not with these."

She laughed as she took both his hands in

hers. "I guess even the best have their lesser moments," she said, settling back on the sofa with him. Ten minutes later she urged him to his feet. "I need to go someplace to breathe. These walls are beginning to close in and if I don't get out of here, I'm going to literally start climbing them. Want to come with me?" she asked, holding her hand out to him. "Maybe go up to the roof garden. It's a good place to think. And be within running distance when he's out of surgery."

Five minutes later, after stopping at the OR desk to let the nurse know where they'd be, Michi and Eric pushed through the door to the garden and stepped outside. It was a beautiful autumn afternoon. The temperature was perfect, but the skies threatened rain. For a moment she felt...peaceful. "This is nice," she said, shutting her eyes simply to enjoy a bit of communing with everything surrounding her. "Back home, I don't have any kind of garden with my condo, so I always enjoy my version of this. Simple things. Plants and sky. And in my hospital garden a little water feature with a foot bridge, lined by cherry trees and bamboo."

Stepping closer to Eric, she laid her hand in the small of his back, not to massage but merely to let him feel her presence, and take whatever strength she had to give. Because he looked exhausted. Strung out. In emotional agony. "Is there anything you want to tell me?" she asked.

"Like I said, Riku's holding his own." Eric turned to look at her. "It's me who's not doing so well. When it's a child you don't know, it's difficult enough, but when it's your own child..." He took in a deep breath, then it was she who pulled him into her arms for a change. She who held him. She who felt his tears on her shoulder.

They stood that way for several minutes before he straightened up, scrubbed his face with his hand and took in a deep breath. "I was doing just fine, staying objective. Until his chest was open and it was my son's tiny heart I saw beating in there. I'm just glad he wasn't awake to see what a mess his old man was."

"But you stayed."

"Because I had to. There wasn't another choice. That was my boy…our boy. This was the first real thing I've been able to do for him and I wasn't going to let him down. It's also when I realized that I'm not my old man, that I don't turn my back on the people who should mean the most to me or, in this case, the child who does mean the most to me. My dad would have walked out. Come back later to see how it turned out. But I'm not my dad."

"You're certainly not," she said, sidling up to him so their arms touched, then eventually leaning against his chest as his arm slipped around her shoulder. "You're certainly not." A tear trickled out of the corner of her eye and blotted itself against Eric's green scrub shirt, leaving its presence there in a damp circle above his heart. "So Henry repaired the truncus?"

"He did, and when I left he was working on the valve to fix some regurgitation that wasn't diagnosed before. That's probably what they're doing now…the surgical creation of a tricuspid truncal valve. In the cases where I've done it, it seems to provide the best outcome."

"You gave them permission for that?" she asked. "Because it wasn't mentioned in the surgical risks that were addressed."

"I did give permission. There are other ways to go about the repair, but in my experience this was the best and will serve Riku better in the years ahead. Should I have spoken to you first?" he asked.

Michi shook her head. "I told you I trusted you to make the right decisions. I'm glad you were there to do that." She pulled back and looked into his eyes. "I trust *you*, Eric. And maybe that's been slow to happen, but it's happened in a huge way. It makes me feel better. Gives me hope I haven't had…ever, simply letting go and trusting. It's easy to be overprotective and not so easy to let someone else in. But I want you in, Eric. I don't think either of us is in a position to know how yet, but just know I do want you in."

Eric nodded, and pulled her even closer. "You've done a very good job taking care of him, and I don't blame you for being overprotective. I would have been, too. And I do want to be in. In his life, in yours… We'll figure it out when the time's right."

CHAPTER NINE

"ERIC," AGNES SAID, stepping out into the garden, interrupting the solitude there. "Michi. I need to talk to both of you."

Eric swallowed hard. This was the part he always hated. The part where either he would step out of surgery to break the bad news, or one of his surgical associates would do it. Judging from Michi's still relaxed body in his arms, she hadn't figured it out yet. But she would.

"Just say it," he said. Too many doctors beat around the bush. He wasn't in the mood for that. He wanted to know what was going wrong, and he wanted to know now. If only he could shield Michi from it. But he couldn't.

"Say what?" Michi asked.

"We haven't succeeded in getting him off the machine." Agnes stepped closer to Michi, but Michi squeezed herself tighter into Eric's arms as if pulling away from Agnes was pulling away from the truth. And getting closer to Eric was getting closer to the only person who could make her feel better right now. "Henry sent me to tell you."

"Which means?" she asked, even though she knew.

"Which means it's going to take a while longer than we expected."

"Any arrhythmias?" Eric asked.

"No, and no excessive bleeding either. He's doing well overall, but he just doesn't want to come off bypass yet. Thought you'd want to know why the delay."

Michi looked at Eric for an explanation. "Is there anything that should be done?" she asked him.

"Trust the man who trusts the surgeon. If Henry's not upset by this—and I'm assuming he's not or he would have called for me—then I'm not."

"Then I'm not either," she said, trying to muster a brave smile that simply wouldn't come.

"Anyway, I'll keep you informed," Agnes said, heading back to the door. "Oh, and, Michi, you've been cleared to sit with Riku in Recovery for a little while. Someone will give you a fifteen-minute warning when the nurses decide it's appropriate."

She nodded her gratitude then went to the ledge surrounding the garden and looked out over the afternoon activity down below. "Down there, everything is so normal. People living their lives the way they were meant to. And us, up here, our lives stalled or even stopped. It doesn't seem fair, does it?"

"Usually, it's not. But we muddle through, don't we? Because, if we don't, what's the alternative?" While he'd always felt cheated and frustrated that he'd left his surgical practice to take up his father's dream, this was the first time he'd actually felt guilty. It was an odd reaction, and it surprised him, and it was also the first time he'd seriously wondered if he could go back to the life he wanted and not the one expected of him. He'd always thought of changing his path as permanent but, as he was discovering, there were unanticipated twists and turns that made life different. And better. But to be a surgeon again… "How about I go talk to Henry, then let you know exactly what's going on?"

"Would you, Eric?"

"Meet me back here in thirty?"

"Can you make that twenty?" she asked.

She looked up at him, then nodded. "Tell him I love him, Eric. Please, tell Riku."

"I will," he said, his voice raspy. "I promise, I will."

Michi was concerned but not upset as she sat outside alone, her back to the garden wall. There was still plenty of light left in the day and, optimistically, by the time it was dark, Riku would be settled in his PICU bed, and all the worries of the world would be long over. It had been nearly twenty minutes already, and she was ready for Eric to return now that she had her second wind and her nerves weren't quite so on edge.

"Want some company?" he asked, coming

up to her, handing her a bottle of water and a tissue, pre-emptively.

She nodded, choking back her tears then dabbing her eyes with the tissue. "How is he?"

"He's fine. On his way to Recovery." He slid down the wall next to her and pulled her into his arms. "They want about thirty minutes to get him settled in then you can see him. Henry's anticipating about two, maybe three hours in Recovery then back to the PICU. He's good, Michi. Strong. Everything that should be taking place now is taking place. He's breathing on his own. His vitals are normal. His heart is beating the way it should, and nothing but normal is showing up in the EKG tracing. It's everything we could have asked for."

"And the bypass machine?" she asked.

"Everything good there, too. It took him a little longer to come off than it usually does, but there really wasn't a reason. Just one of those things."

She leaned over against Eric and lowered her head to his shoulder. It was a safe place to be. A place she trusted with a man she loved. "So now we wait?"

"Yes. And maybe bask in the moment. He sailed through and he's good. I really want to stay in this place for a little while and just be grateful."

"Thank you," she said, wiping back her tears and sniffling.

"Thank you," he said on a deep sigh.

"For what?"

"For Riku. Thank you for Riku."

Michi nodded as words failed her then she collapsed into Eric's arms. "I don't even know what to think," she said. "It's been so long..."

"Then don't think. Merely enjoy the moment. He came through it, Michi. We all came through it."

Light rain was beginning to trickle down when he took her in his arms. They were still sitting on the cement, caught somewhere between the happiness of the moment and the pent-up emotions that no longer needed to be trapped. Riku was on the good side now, the place that made all the difference in the world, and all she wanted was to sit here, getting wet, and feel Eric's arms around her.

"Are you sure we shouldn't go in?" he asked.

"Not just yet. I don't want to share this moment. It's ours, Eric. Only ours. And a little water can't take it away from us, but the people on the other side of the garden door can. If you don't mind sitting here with me for a little while longer." She tilted her face to the sky and let the gentle rain wash over her. "It's funny. I wasn't sure what I'd do at this moment. I had fantasies of jumping up and down or simply crying. But what I want to do… The only thing I can see myself doing is…"

Eric chuckled. "What?"

Michi twisted in his arms to see the glorious rain streaming down his face. "Kissing you."

"Would that be a kiss of gratitude or relief?"

"No," she said, feeling so light she was afraid the churning of the air around her might pick her up and blow her out of this dream. But it wasn't a dream. For the first time it wasn't a dream. "And after the kiss I want you to allow me the chance to tell you that I love you more than I have ever imagined that I could love anybody. It's not going to be simple, and I don't even know how you feel about me, but that doesn't matter, Eric. After you kiss me, I'm going to tell you I love you."

"Then I suppose I should get to that kiss," he said, taking her face between his hands. "Because I like the sound of what comes next." With that, he pressed his mouth to hers. Gently. Ever so gently. It wasn't the kiss of lust or urgency but one of something deeper, of pure need that exceeded the physical.

It was Michi who parted Eric's lips, seeking more than either of them expected. Tongue touching tongue, breathing in rhythm with one another... She wasn't forceful either. More like she simply needed to be there, doing what they were doing, drawing from each other, giving to each other.

She giggled and pulled back when the water from his wet hair dripped to her nose. Then threw her arms around his neck and drew him back into the kiss. But this time it was deeper. A kiss that could lead elsewhere and might have had her cellphone not dinged a text message. "Maybe this is it," she said anxiously as she pulled it from her pocket, while Eric shielded it from the rain.

The message from Agnes was simple. One word. Ready. And that was all it took to catapult Michi to her feet while Eric still sat there on the wet cement. She held out a hand to help him up, and when he rose to his feet he scooped her up into his arms and spun around, both of them laughing and crying. "We did it," she said, feeling like a child let out to play for the first time in her life. The way Riku would soon feel. "We really did it, Eric."

"And…"

She laughed. "Do you really want to hear the words?"

"I do," he said, smiling.

"I do, too." She drew in a deep breath and shouted as loudly as she could, "I love you, Eric Hart." It was improbable, maybe even impossible, but at that moment she needed to say it as much as he needed to hear it. Then, like everything else between them, they'd tuck it away and work out the details later.

"And I love you, too," he said, a little more quietly. Then kissed her as he lowered her to the ground. "Now, go dry yourself off and get to Recovery. Someone there needs you."

"Someone right here needs you," she said, sliding her hand from his as she walked away. "And, yes, I know. We'll sort that along with everything we'll be sorting. But... I just needed to say it. Something I haven't been good at doing."

"And I needed to hear it." He pointed to the door. "Now go. Before I really do pick you up and carry you."

She did go, smiling all the way down to the dressing room to find dry scrubs, then all the way to Recovery. For the first time since that night with Eric, she felt like there was something to hold onto. She needed that in her life. She truly needed that, and Eric was the only one who made her feel that way. She hoped, after the craziness of the past several minutes, that it didn't wash away with the rain.

* * *

It was like the weight of the world had finally caught up to him and crushed him beneath its ugly shell. He was physically tired, emotionally drained, and he had no one to turn to but Michi. Yet as he watched her walk toward the recovery room he was so proud of the strength she was exuding. She'd been through so much more than he had, and for so much longer. But she wasn't broken. Tired. Worn down. But so strong. And it was from her strength that he was finding his own.

"Your kid's a fighter," Henry said, putting his arm around Eric's shoulder.

"He gets it from his mom," Eric commented, his eyes still focused on Michi until she disappeared into the recovery room.

"I know it's none of my business, but what happens now?" Henry asked. "And I'm only concerned because he's my patient."

"You're concerned because you're nosy, you old buzzard," Eric said, chuckling.

"Some of that, too."

"Eventually, when he's ready to travel, he'll

go home to Sapporo. He has good doctors there so I don't think his health is a concern. And when the next surgery is up, well…maybe you again."

"Then you'll fly me to Japan on that fancy plane of yours?"

"If that's what it takes."

"Will you be living there, too, Eric?"

"Michi and I get to a certain point then we don't go any further. As in making plans for what happens next. So, I don't know where I'll be. Probably either going to or coming from Japan."

"Consider staying, Eric. Be with your family there. Maybe get back to surgery."

Eric turned to face his mentor. "Sounds simple, doesn't it?"

"It can be, if that's what you want. Hell, I never thought I'd leave Texas, but look at me now. All small-town New York because the woman I love was worth the change. Anyway, I'm going to have Riku brought back to the PICU as soon as possible so you and Michi can both sit with him. But it's probably going to be three hours, according to hospital protocol. So go rest up. You've got some pretty important daddying to do. Oh, and you're welcome in Recovery, too."

Eric shook his head. "She needs this."

"Well, whatever suits you. See you in a while, when he's back in PICU."

The minutes with Riku flew by then suddenly she was alone in the hall, walking back to the waiting room to find Eric. Riku was still sleeping, and he looked so tiny and fragile against all the machines surrounding him. But his heart tracing looked good. Better than she'd ever seen it. And the blue tinging around his lips these past few weeks had pinked up nicely, as had his fingernail beds. Meaning his heart was working the way it should and his body was no longer being robbed of oxygen.

It was all good, and she couldn't wait to find Eric, wondering if their earlier celebration could be continued, or perhaps had it been a one-off? A reaction to the moment, to the joy, to the relief? So much of this was because of him, and there weren't enough ways in the world to give him the thanks he deserved.

But would he even want to see her now? Especially after the way she'd been so giddy in the garden, saying things she otherwise might not have said, doing things she might otherwise not have done? Well, there was only one way to find out, wasn't there? Go find Eric and simply ask if there was another step for them to take together. Something that would lead to another step, then another…she hoped.

"Isn't Eric here?" she asked her mother, who was sitting near the window in the waiting room.

"He stopped by for a couple of minutes, told us more detail about how the surgery had gone. We thought he'd stay with us, of course, but obviously he didn't. I don't think he knows where he belongs, Michi."

Of course he didn't. She'd never given him the opportunity. Never given him the chance to find out. Or the support he needed as badly as she did. Everyone in Riku's life had their defined place. Everyone but Eric who, while he wore the title of father, was still unsure of where it got him. Did he think that now the surgery was over, he was no longer needed? How could he feel anything but that, when she'd been the one to do that to him?

"I, um… I'm going to take a walk," she said. "Riku's going to be in Recovery for a while longer and I'd really like to get out of here for a bit. They'll text me when he's ready to go to PICU, and I'll be back for that." And while the cafeteria wasn't necessarily her destina-tion, she headed in that direction, hoping to find Eric there. Texting him as she walked.

Where are you?

Lobby. Waiting for my driver. Going home for a while.

May I come with you?

She was not sure why she responded that way but being with Eric was the only thing that made sense. So, she waited for his rather prolonged response before she took another step in any direction.

Sure. Waiting in lobby.

She was positive that his hesitancy in responding right away was because he wasn't sure what to do. And the lack of enthusiasm in his response probably indicated the same. But she was not going to be deterred. They'd put off everything until after Riku's surgery, and now it was after Riku's surgery, which meant it was time to see what they had together in all this. It might not be easy, and it might be heartbreaking, but she'd done a bad thing by Eric once before, and she wasn't going to do that again.

"That white stretch out there is yours?" she asked, stepping up behind him.

"Technically, it belongs to the company, but since I own the company..."

She took hold of his arm. "Care to give me the grand tour? I've never been in a car like that before."

Eric chuckled as he led her out the door. "Let's see, tires, doors, seats inside. And William. When he retired from the company, he wasn't ready to call it quits so I took him on as driver, estate handyman, gardener, whatever. He lives in the guesthouse and he's grateful that even at his age he still has a purpose."

"We all need a purpose, Eric," she said, climbing into the back seat and dropping down into the buttery white leather. "But sometimes finding the right purpose is difficult. Sometimes it takes a few misfires to get it right."

The sky was clear, the rain long gone, and the night was decidedly colder than previous nights. Which meant winter was setting in. And this winter she had plans for Riku. Nothing strenuous, nothing outside except some easy sledding on a very limited basis. Still, for the first time ever she had plans that would happen. Something to look forward to and get excited about. Something so tangible she could almost feel it right now. Before today, all plans had been subject to change, or had disappeared altogether. But not anymore. This was the first time she felt free enough to think forward. "So, you live in the city?"

"Secluded area. Not central but nice."

"Let me guess. Passed down from generation to generation."

"To Riku, when it's time." He settled in across from her and sighed. "Oh, and for what it's worth, white isn't the color I would have chosen. Neither was a stretch. But..."

"It was passed down to you with everything else."

"And Riku can have it right now if he wants it. Personally, I prefer my SUV. But sometimes a Hart has to be a Hart."

"Why tonight?" she asked him.

"Long-range plans involved. And that includes the whole Hart legacy. It only seems proper that it all begins in the Hart stretch."

They drove several blocks before they cut out of midtown and headed for the mansion. This was really the first time Michi had ever explored Manhattan by night, and it was beautiful. Everything she'd imagined. All the magnificent buildings with all their magnificent light. "Would you believe I've never been up the Empire State Building? I think I'd like to go on a clear night, so I could look out on all the lights for miles."

"Then we'll do that. And as Hart Properties has a helicopter, maybe you'd like a ride over the city at night as well. Best view in town, in my opinion."

"Are you a pilot?" she asked.

"As a matter of fact, I am."

"Then you could take us."

"Or I could have the company pilot take us so we could snuggle up in the back seat."

She smiled at the suggestion. "I like that. Bring a blanket, bring a Thermos of hot chocolate."

He chuckled. "Except the chopper is heated, and it's equipped with a coffeemaker, which can easily convert to hot chocolate."

Michi laughed. "You really do know how to spoil the romantic moment, don't you?"

"Old habits that haven't died, I suppose."

"Could we work through them together?" This wasn't what she'd intended to talk about.

At least not now. But she'd declared her intentions without anything back from him. So, she had to know if she was kidding herself, that maybe he was still angry and wouldn't get over it. Or if he was ready to move on, as he'd hinted.

Unfortunately, before he had time to respond, the car had come to a stop outside a virtual castle, and the driver was already opening the door for her to exit. She stepped out, trying not to gawk too much or, at least, with her mouth hanging open, waited for Eric to come from the other side, then took hold of his arm and let him lead her into the most magnificent foyer she'd ever seen. One that belonged on the pages of an architectural journal.

"This isn't what I pictured," she said. Everything was in grand style from the massive pendant lights at the entry to the marble staircase inside the hall. Even the ebony grand piano in the music room off to the side of the entry, the mahogany antique Chippendale chairs sitting across from it, and the heirloom Persian rug upon which everything sat. "It's so…"

"Ostentatious," he supplied.

"Maybe. But beautiful. Like in a museum."

"Or a mausoleum. My dad never let me come in here. I was restricted to my bedroom, my playroom and the kitchen. Occasionally the dining room, when he didn't want to eat alone. Which was hardly ever."

"Too bad, because beauty like this should be enjoyed. Not restricted. Who did the decorating?" she asked, as she brushed her fingers lightly over a sofa table behind the massive empire sofa sitting off to the side of the room.

"A couple of great-grandmothers back, so I'm told. The Hart family has always been larger than life, and their lifestyle was part of it."

"But not your lifestyle?"

"I prefer to keep things simple."

"Yet look at all this. I can't even picture you rambling around through all the halls here, let alone living in them."

He chuckled. "I don't. Pretty much I live in the same area I always have. My bedroom, changed to fit a man rather than a boy. My playroom changed into an office. And the kitchen, where I usually stand over the sink to eat, when I eat here. Which is hardly ever, since I'm more of a grab-bag-and-go kind of a guy."

"Fast food?"

He shook his head. "Top restaurants are more than happy to put a decent meal in a bag for me to take away."

"Well, I'd like to say I'm getting mixed signals on your lifestyle, but I'm not."

"Because pathetic isn't a mixed signal," he said.

"Well, if this was the house I had to come home to, I'd probably live the way you do. All this is good for show, but when it comes to living, I like livable. Someplace where I'm comfortable. A house where, if I break a vase, I can replace it rather than have to claim it on my insurance." She turned back to Eric. "Are you happy here, Eric? I guess that's what's important, isn't it? Being happy where you are?"

"I've never really thought about it. This house exists, and I exist inside it." He sat down at the piano and opened the lid over the keyboard. Then played a perfect arpeggio with the fingers of a perfected pianist. Or a perfected surgeon.

"That's beautiful," she said. "What comes after it?"

"Anything you want. Maybe an old Beatles tune?" With that, he launched into one of the oldest. Then transitioned into Chopin. "A nocturne is always good, too." Then a show tune, followed by several fragmented jazz chords, ending in part of Beethoven's "Ode to Joy" from his ninth symphony. "It's a matter of mood, I suppose."

"And what's your mood?" she asked, taking her place behind him then leaning over and, with one finger, playing a simple melody that sounded Japanese. And haunting. "It's called 'Takeda Lullaby.' My grandmother used to sing it to me. It's an old cradle song sung by burakumin, a group who were outcasts because of their occupations, like undertakers, butchers or tanners. They were deemed tainted by the old society because of who they were."

"And you sing this to Riku?"

"It's one of his favorites. Makes him smile. It talks about rising above adversity to a higher life."

"I think my mood might be like Riku's when he hears this. Not because of the song as much as the way you make me happy."

She changed her tune to the old Shaker hymn "'Tis a Gift to Be Simple" and Eric chuckled.

"Simplicity hasn't ever been anything I've had much to do with in my life," he said.

"Have you ever wished for it?" she asked, as she sat down next to him and continued playing, but with both hands.

"Most of my life. Closest I ever got was when I was in university, but even then, instead of living in the dorm room the way most students did, my dad bought me an elaborate townhouse off-campus."

"And you turned it down, of course, in search of the simpler."

He chuckled. "No, I kept it. But I did turn down the chauffeur and maid that came with it."

"You accept your wealth quite well," she

said, lifting her hands from the keys. They were sitting much too close together, side pressed to side. But it felt so good, so natural that she didn't want to move. Not yet. "Have you ever considered donating your house and all its antiques to a museum and going back to your townhouse days?"

"I have, but something always stops me when I get close to going through with it."

"What?" she asked.

"My sense of family, I suppose. My dad wasn't that great, but there have been other Harts here who weren't him. I remember my grandmother sitting in her room, crocheting. Actually, I remember seeing a picture of her there. She was gone long before my time, but in the photo…she looked so happy. So contented. Getting rid of this house would be getting rid of that. Or maybe the image of another Hart in another photo I've yet to find. So I stay. Keep the part of it I want and leave the rest of it to its posterity. Which probably makes no sense whatsoever. But Riku's now part of that, so the choices will one day be his to make. Or, like me, not make."

Michi stretched her neck and sighed. "It's hard to think that my son belongs to all this. My family is of means, but not on this scale." She stretched her neck again, then laughed. "Too many hard chairs and strange beds lately."

With that, Eric left the bench then took his place behind her and began to massage. "I know this is part of what you do, and I'm sure I'm not nearly as good at it, so guide me if I go wrong here."

She let out a contented sigh. "Trust me. What you're doing is perfect." So perfect, she leaned her head back against him, took in another deep breath and relaxed. This was a touch she wished could be only for her. But that was merely a dream. The reality was that all too soon she would return to her reality and the ache would return, and everything inside that was relaxed now would only tense up again. But for the moment…

"A little to the right," she said, almost on a

moan. "And harder. I can take more pressure. And your thumbs…pure heaven."

"I think that's the first time anybody's complimented me on my thumbs."

"Oh, I think you have a whole lot of body parts to compliment. Remember, I saw them." And behind her shut eyes she was seeing them again.

His massage deepened a bit. "I remember," he said, sighing. "I do remember."

"I think we should stop," she said. Wishing that weren't the case.

"Afraid we could turn this into our second night?"

If only he knew how much she wanted that. Tonight. Right now. Even on the Persian rug. But she couldn't. If they were to happen again, and she truly hoped they would, it had to be perfect. And with everything resolved. Not now, though, as nothing was perfect, and nothing was resolved. Because if ever they were to be together again, she could not bear him leaving her yet another time. Still nothing guaranteed that he would stay. "Yes," she said simply, even though she didn't pull away from him as she might have at one time. Instead, she let him continue his massage as she continued her daydream. For now, anyway. Then, maybe later on...

CHAPTER TEN

MORNING CAME SLOWLY, and the aches and pains from sleeping in the recliner next to Riku's bed were testament to that. Her frame was small, and it felt like the chair had mangled her. She looked over at the next recliner, surprised to find Eric there. He must have come back sometime in the night, even though he hadn't said a word to her one way or another what he would do.

The night had gone so…well, not wrong as much as off track. There'd been so many things she'd wanted to say, wanted to find out and talk about. But the proximity was driving them past the point of normal conversation to a place neither of them wanted to go. Not yet. So she'd returned by cab, made sure everything was as good as it could be in Riku's world, then reread the text from Eric that told her he'd see her first thing in the morning.

Twice after that he'd texted her the sweetest goodnights. So sweet she'd nodded off with a smile on her face. And now here was morning, and she was seeing him first thing, as he'd promised. The excitement of having him there with her caused her heart to do a little flip-flop. Maybe soon they'd be able to wake up the normal way. Wrapped in each other's arms. Glad to be there. Mussed from the night yet ready to make love in the morning.

"Did I miss something?" he asked, his eyes half-shut, waking up about thirty minutes after Michi did.

"Apparently I did—when you came in."

"Didn't want to disturb you, you were sleeping so peacefully. Except for that snore, of course." He looked out the corner of his eye at her. "You must have been tired because it was really loud."

"I don't snore," she insisted behind a giggle.

He scratched his head. "Must have been a

distant fog horn." He chuckled and wiggled his phone in her face. "It records. Just sayin'."

"You wouldn't dare," she said, snatching it out of his hand.

"Try me and see."

"Why, that almost sounds like a proposition of some sort."

Eric blushed and didn't say a word, which disappointed her. She like their lighter moments. Liked enjoying his humor, liked laughing with him. But their conversation was getting dangerously close to a place he obviously didn't want to go, so she changed the subject. "He'll need a morning bath…just a sponge off. Clean clothes. Breakfast. You're welcome to do any or all of it. Or none of it. But, personally, I find his morning routine a great bonding time."

She wasn't sure what to make of Eric's switch in attitude. He changed back and forth so often she wasn't sure what he really wanted. Time would tell, she supposed. And, as of now, she faced two months of it in New York before Riku would be able to fly home.

Eric finally stood, stretched, and went to the side of the crib. His first action wasn't to assess Riku like a doctor, the way Michi thought he would. No, it was to hold out his index finger to Riku, who immediately grabbed hold. "It gives them confidence," he said, holding out his other index finger to Michi. "Glad I didn't bother you last night because you were sleeping so soundly and peacefully. I tried hard to be as quiet as I could."

"I wasn't sure if you'd come."

"I wasn't sure if you'd want me. But I had to come, Michi. Had to take the risk because you and Riku are…everything."

"I gave our situation some thought, Eric. Where your place should be with Riku, where my place should be with you, and yours with me."

"And?"

"And I wonder why we're both so afraid to come right out and admit what we want. Is it because I was accused of trying to harm Riku, or because you were rejected by your father? These things shouldn't shape us, Eric. We shouldn't allow them to, yet they keep coming back to haunt us, don't they? Me afraid you'll see something in me that makes me look like a bad mother. You afraid you'll turn out like your father."

Offering his finger was the first overture he'd made since sometime yesterday—she was too tired to remember when—and she was glad of it. It didn't mean much, but it was a start. So, as she stood there holding on, she felt the connection, and there was nothing tentative or tenuous about it. The three of them... they were a family. Did Eric feel it, too? "He wants to be picked up and held. Doesn't understand why his mommy won't do that since he counts on her for it."

"With all the children I've worked with—the tiny ones, the very young ones—I've always wondered what they think when their world is taken away from them and replaced with all this. You know it's got to scare them to death, but kids are such mighty warriors. They're better at accepting the difficulties than most adults are."

"And Riku is the mightiest," she said, allowing Riku to take hold of her finger, somehow creating a complete bond between the three of them. "I just wish…"

"What?"

"That there was some way through this that wasn't so awkward."

"Everything worthwhile takes time."

"You always make things seem so simple."

"Trust me, they're not." He picked up a soft blue baby cloth and washed areas of Riku that were exposed, then blotted Riku's hair dry. "Especially when you're on the outside, looking in."

"Like you are?"

"Like I am."

She picked up a clean hospital blanket and covered Riku after Eric managed to get him into a small hospital gown. Poor Riku, he looked so frail it broke her heart. So did Eric. But that would change for all of them. Riku would reach his normal weight, gain some strength, and move on like none of this had ever happened to him. She, on the other hand, wouldn't forget so easily. Neither would Eric, judging from the way he looked at Riku.

"He does resemble you, you know. In his eyes. He has kind eyes. And his smile. While he doesn't do it so often, he always reminds me of you when he does. And look at those long fingers…the fingers of a surgeon, per-haps?"

"Or someone who will, eventually, inherit Hart Properties."

"I suppose I never thought of that."

"Well, in my experience, we show him a world full of options and let him decide for himself."

"Because of your dad?"

He shook his head. "No. Because I'm Riku's dad and I want him to have the life he wants, not the life I want for him."

"What about you? What about the life you want?"

"I think I might be in transition again."

"Really? Does that include going back to surgery?"

"It might."

She was so excited she wanted to jump up and down but, instead, she grabbed him and planted a fast, hard kiss on his lips. "That's where you belong, you know. And if there's anything I can do to help you with this… Eric, I'm so happy for you."

"It's not final," he said, trying not to sound too downbeat, at least until he'd talked to hospital admin to see if they'd take him back or not. "Right now I'm just enquiring. And there's the corporation to consider. I've got to put it in competent hands. So…"

"So, if you want it, you'll make it work. You know, what Polonius said."

"What Polonius said." He adjusted the IV tube running to Riku's arm, and by that time Riku was already half-asleep. "Maybe we should go?"

"But he really wants to get out of the crib," Michi told Eric. "And after the doctors make their rounds, maybe I'll be able to do that?"

"Not yet. Riku's got a long recovery period ahead of him, and this is where we all really need to play by the rules. That includes me."

She spun to face him. "Sometimes I hate rules. I wonder who made the rules. Maybe I should go talk to them."

Eric laughed. "Actually, in this hospital, when it comes to pediatric cardiac surgery, I made the rules."

"Seriously? You made rules that hold me back from my son?"

"Seriously," he said, smiling.

"Then maybe you need to go back to being a surgeon just so you can change those rules or modify the penalty if I choose to break them. Because that's what I'm going to do, Eric. Break your rules."

"Somehow I never thought you wouldn't." He bent down, picked up a very squiggly Riku and placed him in Michi's arms. "And if anybody catches you, I'll deny everything."

"Except holding him right after I do. You're not going to deny yourself that, are you? So, while we're breaking the rules, let's talk about you and me."

"Are you sure you're ready for that?" he asked.

"No. But I'm not sure I'm not ready." She sat in the rocking chair, held Riku close to her chest, and started to rock. "So, where do we begin?"

An hour later, they were still talking, but Eric was the one in the chair holding Riku now. "I don't want to be the dad who's always on the plane, Michi. I want to be the one who's always there."

"Which would have me living in New York. Especially if you go back to the hospital."

"But you don't want to live in New York, do you?"

"Because I have family in Sapporo, Eric. Riku needs them, and I need them."

"And I have no family here."

"I don't want to hurt you again, which is why we have to do this now, before we both go jumping off in wrong directions once more. We have a son in the balance and what we do will always be a part of him. The directions we take, the attempts to be inclusive. Personally, I can give up my medical practice just like that." She snapped her fingers. "And if keeping Riku with his father means relocating to New York, I can do that as well."

"But you don't want to."

"Personally, no. I don't. But for Riku..."

"Would you want me in Japan, Michi? You've come up with ideas, but none have me moving to Japan."

"Because your life is here. Your company, your surgical practice, that mansion. It's a big life, Eric. One you won't have in Japan. And I don't know if that will make you happy. You may think so right now, but what happens in four or five years when you have second thoughts? Or your company needs you again? How do you manage that?"

"If I'm happy where I am, there's nothing to manage. That's all I want for the three of us, Michi. Someplace to be happy, and not necessarily someplace in a geographical place as much as emotional one. For me, it's not about what surrounds me. For you, it is...namely, your family."

"You'd move to Japan for my family?"

"No, for *my* family."

Michi nodded, because she had nothing to say. They'd talked this out until there were no more words to speak. It was difficult, wanting the same thing yet not knowing how to come around to get it. She wanted what was best for him. He for her. And both of them wanted everything good for Riku. So it should have been an easy thing to figure out. But it wasn't, and she was frustrated. "Look, I'm going to take a walk and clear my mind. I'll be back in a few."

But her walk took her no farther than right around the corner, where she stopped and leaned against the wall. And that was where she waged her own mental battle. She loved Eric. She wanted to spend her life with him. She was willing to move to New York for him. And he...loved her on that same level, with the same arguments. The problem was, there was no middle ground here. And they desperately needed middle ground. Something that would build the bridge that would truly carry one to the other. Something other than Riku.

"Do you love me, Eric?" she asked, walking back into the room. Riku was back in his crib now, and Eric was standing at the window, gazing out at the sky. "I know you said you do, but do you really?"

"I fail at love, Michi."

"How?"

"I have women who want me for my money, for my looks, my prestige. But no one who's ever wanted me for me. It's a fact of my life, and for me to tell you I love you would always make you wonder where and when I'll mess it up. Can I stay with it? Forget my past? Move on? Be what I want to be and not what I've always been?"

"Your father?"

"My father. His father. It's all the same."

"Which seals Riku to that destiny."

"No. We can't let that happen."

"But if it's a family predisposition, as you seem to think, how can we stop it? How can we keep him from falling into that same line? Because, according to your logic, he will. It's inevitable."

He turned to face her. "We keep him from

falling into that line by being the parents he needs us to be. Not by being the parents we think we should or should not be."

"And we can do that in a barge or a warehouse flat in Hackney in London, if that's the compromise you want to make to keep us together as a family. The where and how don't matter. But the three of us being together does. When I told you I love you, I meant it. It's been growing, and we haven't exactly had normal time to develop it. But you feel that way about me, too, don't you?" she asked.

"Seriously, Hackney? I wouldn't have expected that of you."

"What do you expect of me, Eric?"

"I don't suppose I know, other than the part where, yes, I do love you, and also that you're the best mom…or mum if we move to London, any child could ever have."

"And there is our start."

"Well, when you make it sound so simple…"

"But it is simple, Eric. We start with what we have and build on that. No couple ever starts out with everything. We have some communication problems. And, yes, some of the past may come back from time to time. But we have Riku, which makes us the luckiest couple in the world. And while he can't be our starting place, he can be our inspiration that when we're good together, we can do great things. We already have."

"And the lady hits one out of the park," he said, smiling.

"Because the lady needs to know."

"Then I'll be honest. I want this, and I need it. And I'm willing to do whatever it takes to make it work, including living on a barge, if that's what works for us. I do love you, Michi, but is that enough? Because, believe it or not, my needs are about as simple as they come.

"I don't want the grand lifestyle. Don't want the things that were important to my father, but I'm always going to live with the fear that I might turn into him. You've got to know that because that fear can cloud my judgment. It did when I wanted to reach out to you so many times in the past. And it's a battle I can't fight alone because I don't see it in myself. Or maybe I always see it in myself, even when it's not there."

"I can fight the battle with you. If you fight the one with me that makes me want to tackle the world alone. I used to think I could do it, but it's hard, and it wears me down. But what happens when I hit my stride again? Because I don't want to push you away like I did before. I want to keep you close, where you belong. What if I can't do that, though?"

"Then you turn to me."

"It really is a big leap for both of us, isn't it?" she asked.

"Maybe if we simply hold hands and walk to the edge of the cliff together..."

"It's a long way down if we mess up."

He chuckled. "I can handle heights if you can because I love you, Michiko Sato."

"And I love you, Eric Hart."

"But, seriously, a barge in Hackney? Maybe we could compromise on a warehouse flat overlooking someone's docked barge."

"You don't like water?" she asked him.

"Actually, I own this yacht..."

"Seriously, a real yacht?"

"Well, a yacht and a sailboat."

"Anything else?"

"Some camels, a few windmills, a lake, a couple of Monets, an Indy race team, a football team…" He smiled. "An old bicycle I used when I was a kid that I'd love to fix up for Riku when he's old enough. Oh, and a pony."

"You own a pony?"

"Not yet, but every kid needs one, don't you think? And if you play your cards right, I might get you one, too."

"And what do I have to do to get this pony?"

"Just love me."

"I do. From the first moment I laid eyes on you. Then after you gave me my miracle…"

"Then if you love me, will you live with me in…?" He grinned. "Not Hackney."

"New York?"

He shook his head. "In the mountains outside Sapporo there's a beautiful little cabin that needs happiness and life breathed back into it. It backs into the most beautiful area in which to ski, a nice trip for the weekend in the winter. A beautiful place to be in the autumn. I want Riku to know that place. To know us as a family in that place. It's part of his heritage, Michi. And it'll be a great place to kick back and let him teach me to speak Japanese."

"Are you sure?"

"Earlier, when I was still a doctor with hopes and dreams, and I'd just met you, I'd wondered if we could be more than a one-night stand. You were this amazing, smart lady who knew her place in the world. And you had so much passion for your medical practice. People respected you. I saw that in the way everyone responded to you at the seminar. And here I was, this loner who might have been good at his job but who wasn't very good at life, hoping that things could take a different turn. Maybe even with you.

"But the turn I got… I don't want to manage the company, Michi. I do my best because that's who I am, but I'd rather be back in surgery. I'd rather be happy in my life and planning a future for the three of us as a family. So, yes, I'm sure. Will you marry me? You and Riku are the only important parts of my life and I don't want to lose you."

"If you want me in your life," she said. "Knowing better than anyone else what a mess I can make of things."

"Not a mess, Michi. Just a temporary misdirection. And I do love you. No one's compared since I met you. And keep in mind this deal comes with a pony."

"Ah, yes, the marriage proposal sealed with a pony. We need to have a serious talk about romance, Eric."

"How about you show me romance, instead of telling me about it? I'm a quick learner."

"I know you are, Dr. Hart. I know you are." Michi wrapped her arms around Eric's neck and whispered, "Lesson one, hospital-appropriate and baby-approved." They both looked down at Riku, who was sitting up watching them. And smiling. Michi's heart suddenly filled until it was almost on the verge of overflowing. She'd gone from being the woman who'd thought she could never have her heart's desire to the one who had a lifetime full of it ahead of her. Two men in her life. A little one and a big one.

Yes, she had everything. And she didn't even need a pony. "So, tell me about that yacht," she said, smiling up at him. "I've always had this desire…"

"Any other secret desires I should know about?" he asked, lowering his mouth to hers.

She snaked her arms around his neck and pulled his face all the way down. "Plenty. And you've got the rest of your life to discover them."

EPILOGUE

ERIC PACED THE floor nervously, as any expectant father would do. Along with him his father-in-law, Agnes, his mother-in-law and Michi. Oh, and Riku. This adoption was a family affair, and what a family it was. Everything he'd always wanted and had never thought he'd have.

"She's almost here," Tamiko Tanaka, their adoption attorney, advised. "Dr. Benedict is bringing her here straight from the airplane, and I've been informed that Mali is doing very well."

Dr. Arlo Benedict, his estranged half-brother. The one he wanted to embrace as family for the first time. The one who'd found Mali and had thought he and Michi might be the perfect parents. He didn't know Arlo yet, but he would. That was a priority, and not one to be put off.

He and Michi had been to Thailand twice to visit Mali since Arlo had first called. She was a beautiful child, full of life. Two years younger than Riku, which meant that they would have their hands full with Riku, now four, and Mali, just turned two. Their decision to adopt had happened almost at the same time they'd married in the hospital chapel, a week before Riku had been released. And now, two years later, it was coming true.

"You do realize that in addition to speaking Japanese and English, you're now going to have to learn enough Thai to get Mali through until she understands the other languages we use?" Michi asked. Basically, a mixture of Japanese and English. "And you're going to owe your brother big time for making the arrangements."

Mali had been an orphan, raised in a communal refuge for wounded elephants in a compound near the village where Arlo lived and worked as the village doctor. She'd simply been abandoned there, probably on the assumption that someone there would look after her, maybe teach her to work with the elephants when she was old enough.

Six weeks ago, after Arlo had asked him if he and Michi wanted to adopt, they'd flown down there twice, and now, almost in the blink of an eye…another miracle child. Life couldn't have been any better. Getting Mali, beginning the road to being a better brother to Arlo, the son his mother had had after she'd abandoned Eric. He wanted that. Wanted the family ties in a way he never had before. And it was beginning to happen.

"Chinatsu called, wishing us well," Michi said, fighting to hold onto Riku. He wanted to run down the airport corridor so he could greet his new sister. And, yes, he could run now. And play light outdoor games. He swam, too. Like a fish.

"She's buying up a rather sizeable chunk of Wyoming, she tells me." He'd hired her to run Hart Properties. She was eminently qualified as a businesswoman and had the same sensibilities he had. So, he'd had no qualms when Michi had suggested her cousin as his replacement.

Maybe she wasn't technically part of the Hart family, but she loved her job, and the company was, once again, in good hands, while his hands were where they belonged, performing pediatric cardiac surgery. Life was better than he'd ever imagined it could be and now that he knew what the support of a good family meant, he was no longer sad for what he'd missed but happy for what he'd gained.

"She's turning it into one of your wildlife preserves. Not your dad's first choice, I would think," Michi said.

Eric gave his wife a playful nudge. "Well, I'm not my dad."

"My sister?" Riku asked, pointing to a long-haired man in outdoor gear headed in their direction, carrying a bundle in a blanket. "Mali," Riku pronounced very deliberately.

"Mali and Uncle Arlo. Can you say Uncle Arlo?" Riku looked up at his dad like Eric had gone crazy, then started tugging at his hand, trying to lead him the direction of Mali. "Are you ready to share your toys with her?" Eric asked, trying to hold him back.

Riku contemplated the words for a moment, then grinned and gave his dad a big thumbs-up.

"Then I say let's go meet your new sister." And, hand in hand, the expanding family walked toward the new Hart member. Eric with tissues in his pocket for Michi, of course. And Michi sniffling well before she took her new daughter into her arms.

"Look what we've done," she whispered to Eric, just before Mali was handed to her. "Just look at what we've done."

He did. Every day. And there was never a moment he wasn't amazed by all the miracles it had taken to get them to this place. His place. His family. The prospect of finally getting to know his brother. And, most of all, having Michi in his life. All of them true miracles indeed.

* * * * *